ROBERT RIGBY

GO!

THE DREAM BEGINS

HARCOURT, INC.

Orlando   Austin   New York   San Diego   Toronto   London

www.HarcourtBooks.com

First published 2005 by Corgi Books/Random House Children's Books UK
First Harcourt paperback edition 2006

Library of Congress Cataloging-in-Publication Data
Rigby, Robert.
Goal!/Robert Rigby.
p.   cm.
Summary: Santiago, a young Mexican American, fulfills his dream of
playing soccer when a chance encounter in inner-city Los Angeles results
in a trip to England to try out for the Newcastle United soccer team.
[1. Soccer—Fiction.   2. Mexican Americans—Fiction.
3. England—Fiction.]   I. Title.
PZ7.R44177   2006
[Fic]—dc22   2005033492
ISBN-13: 978-0-15-205798-5   ISBN-10: 0-15-205798-6

Text set in Sabon
Designed by April Ward

C E G H F D B

Printed in the United States of America

ACKNOWLEDGMENTS FOR *GOAL! THE DREAM BEGINS*

GOAL! original story by Mike Jefferies and Adrian Butchart

GOAL! screenplay by Dick Clement and Ian La Frenais

PRODUCERS Mike Jefferies, Matt Barrelle, and Mark Huffam

EXECUTIVE PRODUCERS Lawrence Bender and Peter Hargitay

COPRODUCERS Danny Stepper and Jo Burn

ASSOCIATE PRODUCERS Allen Hopkins, Stevie Hargitay, Nicolas Gautier, and Jonathan Harris

SPECIAL THANKS TO:

FIFA

Adidas

Newcastle United

FA Premier League

1

LIFE WAS BETTER NOW. Santiago eased his lean, toned body back on the pool lounger and gazed out over the shimmering, clear water.

He adjusted his aviator glasses slightly as the afternoon sunshine beat down from a clear blue sky. Even the crucifix around his neck was hot against his brown skin.

All around was luxury—sheer Southern California luxury. Palm trees swayed slightly in the warm, gentle breeze and water sprinklers played on manicured lawns, forming minirainbows as the sunlight caught the droplets. Beyond the pool, steps led up to a wide terrace and beyond that sat the sprawling mansion itself.

Santiago glimpsed the Aztec tattoo he wore proudly

on the inside of one forearm and his thoughts drifted back. To before. To ten years ago . . .

He sees himself, a ten-year-old boy, dazzling his play-mates in a game of soccer on a dust-dry patch of waste ground down in the poorest quarter of a poverty-stricken Mexican town.

Close to the makeshift playing field, tin shacks sit among overcrowded apartment blocks, their walls plastered with colorful graffiti. Washing lines stretch between the shacks and the soccer-mad kids' game is accompanied by a cacophony of salsa music, shouts, crying babies, and the roar of traffic.

But the boys are oblivious to all this. They think only of their game as they scamper about in the dust.

Santiago is in a class of his own. He takes the ball on his chest, allows it to drop from knee to instep, and in a liquid movement he rounds another kid and slots the ball deftly between two beer crates serving as goalposts.

And then the memory, and the picture, shifts, like a television flicking from one channel to another.

Santiago is sleeping. He feels himself being shaken and he opens his eyes. His father, Herman, is staring down at him.

"Get your things, Santiago."

The small boy scrambles from his bed, rubbing the sleep from his eyes. His grandmother, Mercedes, is lifting his baby brother, Julio, from the cot.

"Quickly, Santiago."

The bewildered ten-year-old grabs his photograph of the World Cup, which he long ago tore from an old magazine, and then dives beneath his bed for his one truly prized possession—his soccer ball.

The mental picture shifts again, fast-forwarding to the inside of a battered truck as it bumps along in total darkness. Santiago and his family travel in silence. Another family and a number of young men are also crammed into the ancient truck. Everyone has handed over the required amount of money for this one-way journey.

A baby starts to cry. A match flares as a young man lights a cigarette, and in the sudden light Santiago sees nothing but frightened faces. He clutches his soccer ball even tighter.

When the truck stops, the weary travelers climb out onto a dirt road, and as the vehicle rumbles and wheezes away they are ordered to follow their two guides through a maze of cactus and sagebrush.

They reach the border. Searchlights, mounted on a U.S. Border Patrol wagon, scythe through the inky darkness. The illegal immigrants run up an incline toward a gaping hole in the high border fence.

Just as Santiago reaches the gap, his soccer ball slips from his hands. It bounces away, downhill. He turns to chase after it, but his father grabs one arm.

"Forget it, it's only a stupid ball," he hisses.

Santiago catches one final, fleeting glimpse of his beloved soccer ball before he is bundled through the gap in the fence and his father urges him to "Run! Run! Run!"

Ten years ago. A long time.

Santiago glanced at his tattoo once more and sighed. He heard footsteps, but before he could turn to see who was approaching, a heavy hand cuffed him, none too gently, across the back of his head.

"Get off there. You want to lose us this job? There's leaves to be cleared from the drive. Go get the blower."

Santiago said nothing. He just got up, grabbed his T-shirt, and shrugged as he walked away to carry out his father's orders.

Sure, life was better now. But not much.

2

THE PICKUP TRUCK was going east on Sunset Boulevard, heading downtown. Santiago and his father were crammed into the open back along with three more gardeners and an assortment of machines and gardening tools—including the leaf blower.

Santiago checked his watch, then unzipped a sports bag and began pulling out his soccer gear. He took off his T-shirt and slipped on a faded striped shirt. The other guys took little notice. It had been a long, hot, tiring day; they were saving their little remaining energy for pulling the top from a bottle of beer when they got home.

As Santiago took out his shoes, with their distinctive red and yellow laces, the old guy sitting opposite decided to show a little interest. "How you guys doing this year?"

Santiago shrugged his shoulders. "Two of our best players were picked up by Immigration. Maybe they'll make it back for the play-offs." He checked his watch again. "That's if we make it to the play-offs. I'm late."

By the time the truck pulled up to the curb, Santiago was changed and ready to play. He jumped over the tailgate and went running off toward the park.

Concrete overpasses towered over three soccer fields and a baseball diamond, all of which were squeezed into an area surrounded by industrial units.

The match had already begun, and as Santiago arrived the *Americanitos'* coach, César, was prowling the touchline, a cigarette dangling from his lips. It was many years since César had played soccer; his potbelly was too big for even the outsize pants he wore. But he knew a good player when he saw one.

"What's the score?" asked Santiago, waving both arms toward the referee in an attempt to attract his attention.

"We're one down, and you're late. Get in there!"

The ball went out of play, and as César tottered off to fetch it, the referee came over to where Santiago was standing and pointed at his legs. "I don't want anyone hurt. No shin pads, no game!"

Shin pads were a luxury Santiago had never quite managed to afford. But the problem had arisen before so he knew exactly what to do. Close to the playing field, a couple of overflowing garbage cans were almost hidden by a pile of discarded cardboard boxes. Santiago grabbed one and tore off two rectangular pieces. From a distance, they could almost have been shin pads.

He stuffed one into each of his socks and looked at the referee. "Okay?"

The ref shrugged and beckoned Santiago onto the field. "Field" was a generous, if loose, description. It was rock hard and almost grass-free, and the corner "flags" were three oil drums and the remnants of an old baby stroller.

But that didn't matter to Santiago. The game was all that mattered. The game was what he lived for.

He jogged to his usual position up front, smiling as he saw the relief on the faces of some of his teammates now that their star player had made his belated entrance.

For a few minutes, Santiago felt his way into the game, moving with speed and grace, making deft layoffs and taking up perfect positions the other *Americanitos* never quite managed to read or exploit. He was way ahead of the game, but not yet fully in it, so he dropped a little deeper.

Then he got his chance. One chance was usually

all he needed. He made some space for himself and collected a hopeful punt out of defense. Almost casually, he rounded one lumbering defender, flat-footed another, and then closed on the goal. From the edge of the box he curled a rising shot past the helpless and astonished keeper. He could almost hear the legendary Mexican commentator Andrés Cantor screaming, "GOOOOAALLLLL!!!!!!"

Santiago worked a night job in a popular and noisy Chinese restaurant. He collected dirty dishes, shifted heavy cans and cartons, took out the trash, and sometimes washed the dirty dishes that the young waiters carried in from the restaurant.

He'd been there for more than six months and several times he had asked the boss if he could become a waiter, because waiters got better pay. The answer was always the same. "No, you not Chinese."

There was no arguing with that, but at least every night he worked, Santiago went home with a little more cash. A little more to add to the savings he stashed in an old sneaker kept at the top of the wardrobe in the bedroom he shared with his young brother, Julio.

After the soccer match, Santiago was running late again. One of his teammates gave him a lift in an old car, and as they pulled up outside his home, he had barely enough time to take a quick shower, change his clothes, and maybe grab a burrito as he left for the restaurant. He didn't like Chinese food—he saw too much of it.

He jumped out of the front passenger seat, slammed the door, shouted, "Thanks for the ride," and walked up the incline toward the house, a single-story building perched on a hillside close to Dodger Stadium.

In the small front yard, Santiago's father and another man had their heads under the raised hood of a pickup truck. Herman gave his son no more than a fleeting glance as he passed by and went into the house.

The voice of a soccer commentator blared out from the TV set in one corner of the cluttered living room. The goals from a Real Madrid versus Barcelona match were being shown, and Santiago's grandmother was watching even more avidly than her younger grandson, who was sitting by her side. There were two soccer fanatics in the Muñez family, and as far as Mercedes was concerned, Santiago ranked number two.

She was up and out of her chair as Real scored their second goal. *"¡Mira! ¿Qué te dije?"* she said. They always spoke Spanish at home. "See the difference since Beckham came back? No one crosses the ball like him."

"Yes, I see," answered Julio. "You mind if I get on with my homework now?"

Santiago stood smiling in the doorway as his grandmother switched off the TV set and asked him her usual questions. "How did you do? You play well?"

"Won, four–two. I scored a couple, should have got another." Santiago nodded toward the window. "What's the deal with Dad?"

"He wants to buy a truck of his own."

"Why?"

"So you can work for yourselves. Your own business, Muñez and Son, eh?"

Santiago reached into his sports bag and brought out his asthma inhaler. He took a quick puff. "That's his best plan for me? The rest of my life with dirt under my nails?"

Julio looked up from his schoolbooks. "There's always plan B."

"Yeah? And what's that?"

"The American Dream. We win the lottery, man!"

As Santiago was about to head for the bedroom, Herman came in from the front yard. He didn't look happy, but then he rarely did; life had never done Herman Muñez many favors.

"So what happened?" asked Mercedes.

"The guy wants too much money."

Santiago made certain he didn't smile as he looked at his father. "That's too bad, Dad."

3

EVEN WHEN HE WAS ON VACATION, Glen Foy took his football seriously. He couldn't help it. St. James' Park, or a park in the San Fernando Valley. Shearer and Company, or a bunch of seven-year-olds. Football was football. It was a serious business.

Glen was staying with his daughter Val, who lived in Southern California with her husband and two young sons. And one of those sons, seven-year-old Tom, was out there on the field while his granddad and mom watched from the touchline, shouting their encouragement.

Only in Glen's case, it wasn't exactly encouragement. "Keep your position, Tom! Stop bunching up, you're meant to be on the wing!"

"Dad!" said Val. "It's not the Cup Final. They're seven years old."

"Best to start 'em young."

Glen's accent was an unusual mix of southern Ireland and the northeast of England. He'd lived in and around Newcastle for most of his adult life. At forty-eight, he'd put on a few pounds since his heyday, but still looked in pretty good shape, especially with his suntan.

On the far side of the field a group of young moms were reliving their cheerleader days.

"Go, Wild Cats, go!"

The young kids swept across the field like a swarm of angry bees, but Glen's grandson appeared to be on the periphery of most of the action.

"Come on, lad! Get in there!"

Val rested one hand on Glen's shoulder. "Easy, Dad. To tell you the truth, I'm not sure Tom's heart is really in soccer."

"Soccer," muttered Glen disdainfully. "Soccer. The game's called *football*." He sighed and turned away. There was a senior game taking place on the adjacent field—a team of Hispanics taking on a tough-looking bunch of Europeans wearing the shirts of the Croatian national team.

One player immediately stood out. The young Hispanic picked up the ball at around the halfway line and then, with a deceptive burst of speed, eased his way first past one, and then another defender before sending a perfectly weighted pass across the field. Glen lost interest in the kids' match.

The young player was dictating the game, frequently making fools of the opposition, while at the same time making his teammates look far better than they were.

Glen slowly edged his way along the touchline, close to where a potbellied Hispanic guy with a cigarette dangling from his mouth stood bawling instructions to his team. But not once did Glen's eyes shift from the young player. Even when he didn't have the ball, he was good. The movement. The runs. The feints and dummies. He collected the ball, beat one player, and was then hacked down by a crunching tackle from behind.

"Aye, aye," whispered Glen. "He won't like that."

But the young player simply got to his feet and gave his opponent a withering look that said, *Is that the best you can do?*

The Croatian defenders lined up in a wall, following the shouted instructions of their goalkeeper. The young player waited calmly with his foot on the ball, gesturing to his teammates to take up positions of their own.

When the referee blew his whistle, it looked for a

moment as though the player would go for a cross. But then, effortlessly, and off just a couple of strides, he aimed for the goal. The ball curved around the wall and powered into the net, giving the stranded goalkeeper no chance.

"Bloody hell," whispered Glen before he realized he was spontaneously applauding.

He walked up to the coach. "Did you teach him to do that?"

The coach grinned through tobacco-stained teeth. "God taught him to do that."

"Bloody hell," said Glen again.

The old bus stood in the parking lot shaded by a small stand of trees. Long ago it would have been a school bus, but instead of being towed off to the junkyard when its school days were through, it had been patched up and custom painted with vivid street scenes. As he waited, Glen studied the artwork and read the word *Americanitos* daubed on the side.

The *Americanitos* came ambling toward their bus in twos and threes, chatting about the game, the goals, the missed chances, the ruthless play of some of the opposition. The star player was alone, his shoes with their distinctive red and yellow laces slung around his neck. Glen went straight up to him.

"You played a blinder."

"A what?"

"You played very well," said Glen with a smile. "Brilliant." He held out his hand. "I'm Glen Foy. I used to play a bit myself." As they shook hands, Glen nodded toward the shoes. "What's with the laces?"

The young player looked a little embarrassed. "For my mother. The colors of Spain."

"Oh, right. Still live there, does she?"

"I don't know where she lives." He obviously wanted to change the subject. "So where did you play?"

"England."

"England! You played for *England*?"

Glen laughed. "No, lad, I played *in* England. Have you ever thought of turning pro?"

Most of the *Americanitos* had climbed onto the bus and some were staring out through the dusty windows, wondering what was going on.

"Pro teams here go for college kids. None of us went to college."

"It's usually exactly the opposite in England; don't get many university graduates in the Premier League. Look, I bumped into a British agent I know on the flight out here. I'm gonna get him to check you out."

He saw the player's doubtful look.

"I'm serious; I think you're worth it. I was a scout

for four years after I stopped playing, so I know what I'm talking about."

The bus driver had started up the engine and the team coach appeared on the steps. "Hey, Santiago, come on! Some of us have homes to go to!"

"Santiago," said Glen. "Santiago who?"

"Muñez. It's Santiago Muñez."

"And when's your next game?"

"Saturday."

"Then I'll see you Saturday, Santiago."

4

BEAUTIFUL YOUNG WOMEN clad in Adidas tracksuits were gliding around the open-air Skybar at the Mondrian Hotel with trays of canapés and drinks. But no one ate too much or drank too much. It was all about being there. Seeing the right people, shaking the right hands. Being seen.

Barry Rankin was always highly visible, almost as high profile as some of the soccer stars he represented. Barry sat at a table on the terrace overlooking the city of Los Angeles with his cell phone at one ear. He was enjoying the brunch reception thrown by Adidas to promote their new range of sportswear, even though this particular transatlantic call was to one of his more demanding and troublesome clients. "Gavin, abroad is not a good idea. Down the line, definite, but not now.

Look, if you went to Real or Inter I'd make a ton of money, right? But I won't do that. I'm putting your interests first, Gavin. I'm thinking of you."

Barry was speaking to Gavin Harris, one of his top clients and a Premiership player anxious to settle a move during the transfer window. Barry listened patiently as Gavin explained exactly why *he* thought he should be plying his trade in La Liga.

A girl carrying a tray was hovering nearby and Barry gestured to her for another drink—only his second. He lifted a glass from the tray, took a sip, and resumed the long-distance conversation. "But think of the drawbacks, Gavin. Foreign country, foreign food, and the only foreign food you like is curry. Believe me, you won't get a good vindaloo in Madrid. Look, you've got to trust me on this. I'm on to it and I'll have it sorted before the transfer deadline. Now, I've got to go; someone here I *have* to speak to. Say hello to Christina. Bye, Gavin."

He ended the call and sat back in his chair. There was no one he *had* to speak to, but there were one or two people he wanted to have a few words with, including the blond who had given him his drink. He stood up and was starting to stroll across the terrace when he felt a hand on one arm.

"Barry, is this a good moment to talk?"

Barry turned round, smiling his most welcoming smile. After all, it just might be Sir Alex Ferguson, the manager of Manchester United.

It wasn't. Barry was confronted with a face he knew from somewhere back in time, though he couldn't quite put a name to that face. But the smile remained; this could be business and Barry was always open for business. "As good a time as any, er . . ."

"Glen. Glen Foy."

"Of course, Glen. What are you doing out here?"

"On holiday, staying with my daughter."

"Nice. Having a good time? It's all a bit unreal out here, eh? La-la Land."

Glen sighed. He'd had a feeling that this wasn't going to be easy. "I phoned you, remember? About the lad I saw playing. You really ought to take a look at him before you go back."

"Of course I remember, Glen. But my life's a meeting, man. I hardly have time—"

"He's a young Mexican kid," said Glen quickly, unwilling to be sidetracked. "They played in second-hand strips on a pitch with gopher holes, but he was special. I'm telling you, he dazzled me, and I don't dazzle easy."

Barry's phone rang. He glanced at the screen and chose to ignore the call. "There's a lot of good young kids around, Glen. And not enough teams for them all."

Glen had been expecting this; it was time to play his trump card. "Last time I was dazzled, it was a young kid called Jermain Defoe. My lot didn't want him, and nor did you."

Barry held up both his hands. "Yeah, yeah, all right. Sore point."

"The lad's playing at UCLA next Saturday. Two o'clock. Will you be there?"

Barry nodded, apparently convinced. "I'll be there. Totally." His phone rang and once again he looked at the screen to check on the caller. "I have to take this one, Glen. Business."

"You will . . . ?"

"I'll *be* there. Now relax. Grab a drink; get yourself some food. Chill."

5

THE *AMERICANITOS* BUS was a lot fuller than usual as it trundled down Sunset Boulevard through glorious Beverly Hills. Today's match was in glamour land, and friends and girlfriends had come along for the ride, to breathe in the heady atmosphere, to feel part of it all. For one afternoon, at least.

Santiago sat at the back with his grandmother and brother. He was staring out through the window and looked nervous and edgy.

Mercedes looked plain angry. She'd been building up to saying something from the moment they boarded the bus, and both grandsons knew what was coming. "Your father should be here to watch you."

"It's just another game," said Santiago with a shrug, sounding a lot more indifferent than he felt.

"It's not!"

Santiago turned to look at his grandmother. "You know what he said when I told him about the agent?"

"I can probably guess."

"He said, 'Movie stars have agents. What does an agent want with you?' So I tell him. I tell him the agent sees me, he signs me, I go to Europe and make plenty of money and I come back and buy us a house on the west side. And you know what he says then?"

Julio had been reading a book, apparently not listening to the conversation. But he looked up and repeated the words they had all heard from Herman many times. " 'There are two types of people in this world. People in big houses, and people like us who cut their lawns and wash their cars.' "

"That's exactly what he said," said Santiago as his brother went back to his book. "The only way he believes we can make things better is by buying a truck so we can have our own gardening business. Big deal."

Mercedes sighed. "Your father has had a hard life."

Santiago glanced at his ripped jeans and faded T-shirt. "And we don't?"

The field was good, better than anything the *Americanitos* had ever played on. The grass was in pristine condition and reminded Santiago of some of the lawns he spent hours cutting. And it wasn't just the field that was different. On either side there was banked seating for spectators and even a proper scoreboard.

On the far touchline, the Galaxy Reserves were getting their prematch pep talk from no less than four identically tracksuited coaches. Nearby stood trestle tables loaded with electric fans, coolers packed with soft drinks, and rows of plastic water bottles. To complete the picture, trim cheerleaders were going through the first of their perfectly drilled routines.

The *Americanitos*—and their girlfriends, proudly dressed up for their day out in their tightest skirts and largest hooped earrings—simply gawked. They'd seen nothing like this before. This was another world.

César, cigarette dangling from his mouth as usual, looked at the anxious faces of his own players as they stared across at the tanned, athletic, all-American boys waiting to take the field.

He spat his cigarette out onto the ground. "Hey, come on, you guys, we gonna beat ourselves here? Okay, they look good, but that don't mean they play good. Get out there and show them what the *Americanitos* can do!"

César's rallying call was answered with a few halfhearted shouts of "Yeah" and "All right," but the portly coach feared that the Galaxy Reserves might have this game won before they even kicked the ball. Even Santiago looked nervous. But Santiago was nervous for another reason: This was the chance he had only ever dreamed of.

Farther along the touchline, he saw a man standing up in the ranked seating. He was waving. It was Glen. Santiago waved back. Glen was here; that must mean the agent was here, too.

As his teammates ran onto the field, Santiago kneeled down by his sports bag, turned his back, and grabbed his inhaler for a quick, unnoticed hit. Only his family knew about the asthma: He preferred it that way.

Glen was sitting with his daughter, and as the teams lined up, his eyes were scanning the spectators for Barry Rankin. He was late.

The match had not started well for the *Americanitos*; they were already one down and were struggling to keep up with a clinical, well-organized side playing disciplined soccer.

It was plain to see the result of the Galaxy Reserves having four coaches. They were neat and efficient in defense, midfield, and attack, and while no one stood out, as a unit they were impressive.

Santiago was playing a lot deeper than he preferred, trying to marshal the midfield, attempting to get something going.

If it was frustrating for Santiago, it was even more so for Mercedes as she watched and fretted with Julio at her side. "They can't keep possession. Santiago is too deep. Too deep. He should be up front."

"If he goes up front he'll never get the ball," said Julio.

On the far side, Glen was worried, too, not only because Santiago was struggling to show his true ability, but also that there was still no sign of Barry Rankin.

There was a rare cheer from the *Americanitos'* supporters and Glen looked back from scanning the seating to see Santiago emerging from a tackle in his own half, the ball at his feet. He rounded an opposing midfielder and set off on a long run out wide. As he cut inside, a defender came thundering into the tackle. Santiago dummied him as though he wasn't there, went wide again, and looked up for support. It was still on the way; there was no one to pass to.

As the fullback bore down, Santiago shimmied inside and sent a left-foot shot from the tightest of angles screaming past the goalkeeper and in at the near post.

"Yes!" shouted Mercedes.

"Oh, yes!" bawled Glen. He turned to his daughter. "You see! That's what I've been talking about. And that pillock Rankin isn't even here to see it! Can I use your phone?"

Barry Rankin had his eyes full elsewhere. He was stretched out on a lounger at someone's—he couldn't exactly remember whose—beach house, admiring the bikini-clad eye candy draped around the pool. Music was pumping out from a CD player and Barry was enjoying a long, cool drink when his cell phone rang.

Without thinking, he flipped it open and answered the call. "Yo!"

He didn't get a chance to speak again for the next thirty seconds as Glen bawled him out for not being at the game.

When Glen finally paused for breath, Barry took his chance. "Listen, Glen, listen. I did *not* forget. I've been in a meeting since breakfast."

"A meeting with music!" shouted Glen.

Barry gestured for the nearest girl to turn down the CD a little. "Just finished, mate," he said into the phone. "I'm grabbing a late lunch. Look, I'm having real trouble tying up this Gavin Harris deal."

"But I've got a kid here who's special. Very, very special."

"Yeah, I know, you said. Can you get me some video on the kid?"

"Video! Are you crazy? Forget it, Barry, and I hope you choke on your late lunch."

Glen hung up and Barry was left holding the phone with no one to speak to, aware that the three closest girls were watching. He smiled and shrugged. "Bad connection."

Thanks mainly to Santiago's inspirational goal and his all-around performance, the game ended in a one–all draw. The *Americanitos* lifted their game in the second half and almost stole the match when, close to the end, their star man thundered a shot against the goalposts.

But a draw was a fair result, and as Santiago joined his grandmother and Julio at the touchline he saw Glen walking toward them.

"You played great, son."

Santiago nodded his thanks. "This is my grandmother and my brother."

"And you are the agent?" asked Mercedes quickly.

"No, Grandmother," said Santiago. "This man arranged for the agent to come."

Glen wasn't looking forward to the next bit, but they had to know. "And I'm afraid he didn't. He let me down. Said it was business, the usual excuses."

He saw Santiago's crestfallen look and felt worse than he already did about raising the lad's hopes.

Mercedes was still optimistic. "So he will come to the next game, yes?"

"I'm afraid not. He's going back to England tomorrow, and so am I. I'm really sorry, Santiago."

Santiago reached down and picked up his sports bag. "I guess my old man is right. You dare to dream, but that's all it can ever be—a dream . . ."

6

IT WAS MEANT to be a farewell barbecue. The family, a few neighbors; everyone gathered together out in the backyard, having a good time, all wishing Glen bon voyage at the end of his vacation. The family was there, and so were the neighbors, but the guest of honor had gone missing.

Glen was inside the house, perched on the arm of a chair in the family den. He was making a transatlantic phone call, waiting impatiently for the call to be answered. Glen felt as though he had let Santiago down.

In his own playing career, Glen had never been a headline grabber, a genius who could bring a crowd to its feet with a flick, or a run, or a stunning volley from outside the box. He was more a workhorse, tenacious, the Mr. Dependable who never gave up.

And he wasn't going to give up now, not while there was still a chance. Slim, unlikely—but still a chance.

The phone was answered and a sleepy voice muttered, "Hello?"

"Mr. Dornhelm, it's Glen Foy."

In Newcastle, Erik Dornhelm heard his wife sigh with irritation as his eyes cleared and focused on the digital clock. It read 3:32. "Glen . . . ? Do I know you, Mr. Foy?"

"I was your chief scout, when you first took over. You fired me—well, not exactly fired me; you wanted your own people. I understand that and I don't hold it against you."

"You don't? So why are you calling me at three thirty in the morning?"

Glen smiled; at least he hadn't slammed the phone down. Not yet. "I'm in California. I've seen a player here. I think he's a remarkable talent."

"And who does this remarkable talent play for?"

"It's just local league, but the thing is, I'm on a plane back home tomorrow and I need you to make me a promise."

Dornhelm's wife turned over and hissed, "Erik!" as she pulled the duvet up over her head.

"Mr. Foy," said Dornhelm quietly. "You're waking me up like this just so I can make you a promise?"

"Yeah. If the lad turns up on your doorstep, will you see him? Give him a run out, that's all I'm asking."

Dornhelm laughed quietly. "That's all, eh? And if I make this promise, can I go back to sleep?"

"Yeah, course you can, Mr. Dornhelm."

"Then yes, Mr. Foy. Good night."

He hung up and Glen smiled. Suddenly the steaks sizzling out there on the barbecue seemed a lot more appetizing.

Santiago and his family emerged from the church into the bright Sunday morning sunlight. The priest was standing by the door, dutifully shaking hands with every member of his flock as they left after Mass.

As Santiago walked down the steps he heard one short, sharp burst on the horn of a Ford Explorer parked across the road. In the rear were the kids and Glen's luggage, and the man himself was sitting in the passenger seat, next to Val.

He waved as Santiago saw him, got out of the car, and came hurrying across the road. "I'm glad I caught you. I called your coach—he told me where to find you."

"The agent?" said Mercedes. "He comes to see Santiago after all?"

"Better than that," said Glen. "Santiago, if you can get yourself to England, Newcastle United will give you a trial."

Santiago stared. "Newcastle! Are you kidding me?"

Before Glen could answer, Herman grabbed Santiago's arm and spoke to him in Spanish. "What is all this? You really think you can go and play soccer in England? It's *bullshit*." He turned on Glen and reverted to English. "Why do you fill him with ideas like this? Who the hell do you think you are?"

He walked away while everyone else squirmed with embarrassment. Everyone but Mercedes, who turned to Glen. "He is supposed to fly halfway across the world on something you say? This is a big thing you ask of Santiago."

"I'm not *asking* him to do it; I'm saying he *should* do it. He's a special talent, and I hate to see special talent go to waste. The Newcastle manager has promised me that Santiago will get a trial. The rest is up to him."

The Explorer's horn sounded again and they looked over to see Val anxiously pointing at her watch and then beckoning Glen to the vehicle.

"I'm gonna have to go or I'll miss my flight," said Glen, reaching into a pocket and bringing out a card. He handed it to Santiago. "That's got my home and business numbers on it. I hope I see you again, Santiago. I really hope so."

Money. Cash. Dollars. As Santiago sat in his bedroom counting his savings that afternoon, he realized his father was right about one thing, at least: The whole world revolved around dollars. The need for them, the quest for them, and, in his case, the lack of them.

He didn't have enough cash to get to England, but as he stuffed the bills back into the old sneaker, he made up his mind he would earn what he needed to make the trip. It would take a little time, but he'd do it.

Until now, Santiago had never quite known what he was saving for; it had just seemed like a good idea. Saving for something, someday. Now he knew exactly why. He had a goal. He was going to England. To Newcastle.

He was about to push the sneaker back into its hiding place in the wardrobe when the bedroom door opened and Julio breezed in, a baseball in one hand and a catcher's glove on the other.

Santiago hurriedly put the sneaker behind his back and sat down on his bed. "Why don't you knock?"

"Because it's my room, too," said Julio, sitting on his own bed. He threw the baseball hard into the glove. "You got enough?"

"What?"

"Santiago," said Julio, as though he were the one talking to *his* kid brother. "Everyone knows you keep your money in that sneaker."

"They do?" Santiago pulled the sneaker from behind his back and sighed. "Can't anyone have a little privacy in this place?"

"Nope," said Julio, transferring the ball back to his throwing hand. "Are you going, then?"

"Grandma thinks I should."

"And what about Dad?"

"I haven't asked Dad. There's no point." Santiago got up and pushed the sneaker back into the wardrobe. As he turned round, his younger brother threw the baseball toward him, just out of arm's reach. Santiago stretched for the ball, but it clipped his fingers and fell onto the floor.

Julio laughed. "You'd better go. You're sure not gonna make it at baseball. How far is England?"

Santiago stooped down, picked up the baseball, and tossed it back to his brother. "Right now, about four hundred dollars too far."

Four hundred dollars: small change to many of the rich folk Santiago worked for, but for him, it was a lot. He just had to get on with it. He started his money-making scheme that evening at the Chinese restaurant, first by asking the boss for every extra shift he could get, and then by employing his own special skills during his first break.

Two of his coworkers stood watching in the alley at the back of the restaurant as Santiago effortlessly played "keep-up" with a soccer ball.

"Yeah, very pretty, Santiago," called one of them. "But that ain't gonna take my money."

"Nor mine," yelled the other young Latin American. "And don't let it touch the ground. You said, without touching the ground."

Santiago smiled, and lifted his head for a moment as he measured the distance. Then he flicked the ball a little higher with his right foot and just before it touched the ground he brought his foot through and sent the ball into the air. It came down exactly where it was meant to, into a trash heap more than fifty feet away.

"That's five bucks each," he said as his friends dug into their pockets for the cash.

In the days that followed, Santiago worked harder than he ever had. He didn't mention his plan to his dad; he just cut grass, cleared leaves, dug flower beds, and, most boring and exhausting of all, cleared brush, hacking away at dead undergrowth with a machete. Whatever the job, however tiring, he got on with it, without complaint. And every evening, as his day's pay was counted out into his hands, he mentally calculated how much closer he was to the four hundred dollars he needed.

His dad would watch, but say nothing.

Santiago's only relief from the grueling routine was when he played for the *Americanitos*. That was never hard work; soccer was what he lived for.

He was usually dropped off outside the house after matches. And as he jumped from the bus after one weekend game, he noticed a pickup truck parked close to the house. It wasn't new, maybe five years old, but it had obviously very recently been cleaned up and made to look its best.

At first, Santiago thought nothing of it, but then as he got closer he saw what was loaded into the back of the truck. The lawn mower, hoses, the leaf blower, garden forks and spades. Santiago recognized them all.

Then he realized. Then he knew.

He sprinted for the house, through the front door, past both his grandmother in the kitchen and his father, who was sitting watching television.

Santiago dashed into his bedroom and threw open the wardrobe door. His hands were trembling as he reached for the old sneaker. It was still there, but as he pulled it down and looked inside, he saw exactly what he had feared. Nothing. The money was gone.

For a few moments Santiago stood perfectly still, trying to stay calm, trying to keep his breathing regular. Then, with the sneaker still in his hands, he went back to the living room.

His father looked up from the television as he felt Santiago's eyes boring into him.

"You took it. How could you do it?"

"I paid forty-five hundred for the truck," said Herman loudly, before Santiago had the chance to say any more. "From you, I take twelve hundred, but I'm giving you half the business. That's a good deal!"

Mercedes came to the kitchen doorway. "You took his money? You stole it?"

"Stay out of this, Mother!" said Herman, getting up from his chair.

"You knew what the money was for!" yelled Santiago, unable to stop himself from shouting. He threw the empty sneaker onto the floor. "Two more weeks and I would have had enough!"

"To chase your stupid dream!" Herman's face was red with anger. "Big-time soccer player in England! It's bullshit! And when you fail, how you gonna get back in this country without papers?"

"I won't fail! You think I should give up, just so I can do what you do!"

They were glaring at each other, eyes bulging, fists clenched. Herman took three steps forward, until his face was just a few inches from his son's. When he spoke, his voice was deep and low as he struggled to suppress his fury. "What I do? I'll tell you what I do. In Mexico, I worked day and night to get us to America. When your mother walked out on us, I held this family together!"

"Leave my mother out of this!"

Santiago started to walk away, but his father grabbed his arm. "I worked. I made enough to get us this house. Now we have our own business, everything gets better."

"For you!" said his son, shaking himself free. "But not for me!" Santiago looked at his grandmother, who sighed and shook her head. They both turned away. Mercedes went back into the kitchen and Santiago returned to his bedroom.

His chest felt tight. His breathing was shallow. He pulled open the drawer in the cabinet next to his bed and took out his spare asthma inhaler. He needed it. Badly.

7

NEWCASTLE UNITED CHAIRMAN Freddie Shepherd looked happy. Barry Rankin looked happy. Gavin Harris looked happy. And Erik Dornhelm was making sure he looked happy.

He *was* happy. For the most part. The club's new signing was good; there was no doubt about that. For £8.4 million he had to be good. As the second half of the season's push for that vital Champions League spot gathered momentum, a skillful, attacking, goal-scoring midfielder was exactly what the team needed.

Gavin Harris was all of that. And a bit more. He came with history, a playboy reputation. There had been several unwelcome appearances on the front pages of the tabloids to offset the many back-page reports of his artistry and match-winning performances.

Signing Harris was a gamble, but if it helped clinch that Champions League place, it was a gamble both Freddie Shepherd and Erik Dornhelm were prepared to take. Dornhelm was no pushover as a manager; he had a reputation, too, as a tough, no-nonsense disciplinarian.

Gavin Harris certainly looked the part as he sat on the podium, flanked by Dornhelm and Shepherd. His clothes were casual, but top-designer, exclusive, expensive casual.

The club had chosen to unveil their new signing in the conference room of one of Newcastle's top hotels. The three men were all smiles behind the bank of microphones jutting up from the table in front of them. Cameras flashed as photographers jostled for position and reporters fired in the usual questions.

Barry Rankin stood on one side of the podium. His smile was the broadest of all. He had worked hard to finally clinch this deal, harder than his client would ever know. Barry reckoned he deserved every penny of the percentage he would make on the Gavin Harris transfer.

"It's a great honor to be joining Newcastle United," said Gavin in answer to a reporter's question. "Alan Shearer has been a hero of mine for years. I'm very grateful to get the chance to play alongside him in the same team."

Dornhelm nodded and kept smiling. So far, so good: The new boy had said all the right things. Time to wind up the carefully staged event, while they were still ahead.

He got to his feet, holding a pristine black-and-white Newcastle United shirt with the name HARRIS already printed on the back. "This is a very good day for the club. Gavin is a very gifted player; he should fit in very well with our setup. I'm very pleased to present him with this shirt."

Gavin stood up and both men held the shirt as the cameras flashed again.

Dornhelm may have been anxious to bring the event to a close, but some of the reporters had other ideas.

"Winning the league's out of sight, Erik," called one. "What are your realistic goals for the rest of the season?"

"Qualifying for the Champions League. Top European football is essential for a club like this."

Another reporter spoke up from the opposite side of the room. "Then you'll need to start picking up a few more maximum points from the remaining games, won't you?"

Dornhelm was ready with the standard diplomatic answer about the quality of the opposition in the Premiership, but before he could reply, Gavin Harris spoke up. "Shouldn't be a problem." He looked at Dornhelm. "Bring 'em on, eh, boss?"

Dornhelm's smile remained fixed, but he said nothing. In his mind, he could already see tomorrow's back-page headlines running along the lines of: COCKY HARRIS SAYS EUROPE IS NO PROBLEM.

At the side of the podium, Barry Rankin kept smiling as he let out a huge sigh of relief, very glad that the deal was well and truly done.

"Where's your father?"

Santiago stood with his T-shirt in one hand, ready for a quick shower before another shift at the Chinese restaurant. His grandmother and brother had obviously been waiting for him to arrive home and they obviously had something to say. "He's gone to El Monte to get a part for his precious truck. Why?"

"Good," said Mercedes, walking over to the old bureau on one side of the room. "He doesn't have to hear this." She opened the bureau, took out a large brown envelope, and tipped the contents onto the table. "Train ticket to San Diego. Bus ticket to Mexico City."

Santiago almost dropped the T-shirt. "Mexico City?"

"You can't fly to London from L.A.," said Julio. "You're illegal."

Santiago looked from his grandmother to his brother and then back to his grandmother. "What's going on here?"

By way of explanation, Mercedes picked up the third ticket lying on the table. "This is your plane ticket. It's dated one week from now to give you time to get a passport."

"Pass—?" Santiago finally realized exactly what his grandmother had done. "How did you do this? Where did you get the money?"

Mercedes shrugged. "I've worked hard all my life. I have savings."

"*Had* savings," corrected Julio. "And she sold things, too."

"What things?"

Mercedes glared at her younger grandson and then shrugged again. "Things from the past. Don't worry, it's for your future."

"Grandma, I can't—"

"Don't start telling me what you can't do. This is about what you *can* do, what you *must* do."

Santiago looked at his brother. "You knew all about this?"

Julio smiled. "Of course I knew. You're the only one who doesn't know things around here. You have to go, I want the bedroom to myself."

He was putting on a brave face; they all were, now

43

that Santiago's dream of going to England was so close to becoming reality.

"But take a shower before you go," said Julio. "You smell real bad."

"Tonight?" said Santiago to his grandmother. "I'm going tonight?"

Mercedes nodded. "Before your father gets home. You'd better get packed."

Santiago went to his grandmother and brother, put his arms around them both, and pulled them close. All three had tears in their eyes.

"Julio's right," said Mercedes through her tears. "You do need a shower."

8

THE IMMIGRATION OFFICIAL at Heathrow Airport studied the photograph in the brand-new Mexican passport with great care. Then he lifted his eyes and studied Santiago's face with the same care and attention.

Santiago smiled self-consciously. His smile was not returned as the official went back to his close examination of the photograph. He looked up again. This time Santiago didn't smile.

"Purpose of your visit?"

"Excuse me?"

"Business or pleasure?"

"Oh," said Santiago. "Business. Yes, business."

Santiago saw the raised eyebrows and realized that his questioner was thinking that the young man facing him certainly didn't look like a businessman.

"I play soccer. That is, I hope to."

The eyebrows lifted a little higher. "For who?"

"For Newcastle United."

"Is that right? One moment." He turned away and beckoned to one of his colleagues. In the long line behind Santiago, other weary travelers sighed and visibly sagged at the thought of another delay. Many were tired and irritable; their aircraft had landed more than an hour after its scheduled early morning arrival time.

"This young man wants to play for your team, Mr. Henderson," said the official as his colleague joined him at the desk.

Santiago waited as the second man subjected him to another few seconds of close scrutiny. "For Newcastle?" he said at last.

"Yes, sir," replied Santiago nervously.

"You'd better let the lad in, then," said the new arrival in a strong Geordie accent. "We need all the help we can get."

Glen Foy was hard at work. Since losing his scouting job, Glen had built himself a successful business devoted to another of his loves—classic cars. And while no old E-type Jaguar, Morris Minor, or Triumph Herald could ever give Glen the same thrill as that first sight of an undiscovered soccer talent, he enjoyed his work.

He kidded himself that finding old vehicles for restoration wasn't *so* different from scouting for young players. Both jobs required a keen eye, the knack of assessing potential, and the confidence to act quickly to drive away rivals. He knew he was kidding himself, but it helped: Restoring cars was a job; soccer was in his blood.

Foy Motors—Glen hadn't thought for too long about the choice of name—employed three mechanics and a receptionist-cum-secretary, who shared an office with Glen. But the hub of the operation was the workshop, and whenever he could, Glen liked to go out there and get his hands dirty.

He was standing beneath an E-type on a hydraulic lift, checking out the exhaust system, when he heard a female voice shouting over the noise of men at work and the radio which was always switched on. "Call for you, Glen!"

Glen wiped his hands on a convenient piece of oily rag, went to the office, and picked up the phone. "Hello, Glen Foy."

"Glen, it's me, Santiago."

"Santiago!" said Glen, genuinely pleased to hear Santiago's voice. "How you doing, son?"

"I'm good, Glen. Fine."

"This is a great line, you could almost be in Newcastle."

"Not quite. I'm in London—Heathrow Airport."

There was no reply, and for a moment Santiago had a terrible feeling that it had all been a mistake, that Glen had never really intended him to come to England. "Glen? Glen, are you there?"

He heard Glen laugh. "Course I'm here, lad. You took me by surprise, that's all. You did it: You came."

"I want to play for Newcastle."

Glen laughed again. "Then you'd better find your way to King's Cross Station, lad."

It took a couple of hours, but Santiago made it to King's Cross. The station was heaving as thousands of travelers dashed to or from platforms, studied the huge departures board, lined up for fast food, or streamed, like a trail of ants, down the stairs toward the maze of tube lines running deep underground.

Santiago's ticket to Newcastle used up a huge amount of his remaining funds, but he didn't care; the long journey was almost over. He walked onto the platform and climbed into the first carriage of the waiting blue-and-orange Great North Eastern Railway train.

The trip to the northeast of England would take three and a half hours and Santiago was impressed as he threw his bag onto the luggage rack and settled back into the seat. He was going to travel in style:

plenty of legroom, comfortable seat, even a little lamp on the table in front of him. He would relax and enjoy the ride as he took in the beautiful English countryside he'd heard so much about.

The train pulled away and Santiago got his first real view of England: grimy North London streets and Victorian terraces. It wasn't quite what he had been expecting but he guessed it would get better once they made it to the countryside.

As the train snaked its way through North London, Santiago saw the brand-new Emirates Stadium, soon to be the home of Arsenal, close to the track on his right. And then in the distance he could see Highbury, the famous old ground the club would be leaving. Soccer: It was everywhere in England.

A uniformed man came wandering along the carriage asking to see all tickets. He stopped and gave Santiago a slightly suspicious look as the young man dug into his jeans pocket and handed over his ticket.

"Did you wish to upgrade, sir?"

"Upgrade?"

The ticket inspector sighed. "This is a standard ticket; you are traveling in first-class accommodation."

"I shouldn't be here?"

"Not unless you are prepared to pay considerably more than you have for the privilege."

"More?" said Santiago, horrified. "No, I can't pay any more."

"You'll find second-class accommodation in that direction," said the ticket inspector, indicating the front of the train with his thumb.

Santiago grabbed his bag from the rack and passed straight through another carriage just like the one he had speedily vacated. He reached the buffet car and then the first of the standard carriages.

It was easy to see the difference; the compartment was crowded and the seats were much more cramped with a lot less legroom, but as Santiago took the first vacant seat he found, he felt comfortable enough. He was tired, and as the train gathered speed, he drifted off to sleep.

He woke with a start when he realized someone was poking him in the shoulder. For a few confusing seconds he thought he was at home, and that his father was waking him to go to work.

He opened his eyes and saw an elderly woman glaring down at him. "You are in *my* seat, young man."

Santiago shook his head, clearing his thoughts. The train had stopped at Peterborough and new passengers were moving about the carriage. "Your seat? You own this seat?"

A man sitting on the other side of the aisle leaned across toward Santiago. "There's no need to be cheeky. Give the lady her seat, there are plenty more further down the train."

"But I didn't know—"

The woman brandished her ticket in front of Santiago's face. "I have a ticket with my seat reservation printed quite clearly on it. If you look at the card at the back of this seat, you will observe that you are sitting in *my* reserved seat. Do you wish me to call the ticket inspector to get you to move?"

"No! No, no," said Santiago quickly as he stood up and saw the card at the back of the seat. The last thing he wanted was another run-in with the ticket inspector. He grabbed his bag from the rack. "I'm sorry, I didn't know."

"They all say that," said the woman, as Santiago moved even farther toward the front of the train. He felt as though he was gradually walking to Newcastle.

Eventually, he reached a carriage where there were plenty of unreserved seats and he settled down for a third time.

The rest of the journey was uneventful and the view got a lot better. The train stopped at stations with unfamiliar names like Doncaster, York, and Darlington, and after three hours it pulled in to Durham.

As it moved away again, a voice came over the PA system to announce that the next stop would be Newcastle.

Santiago felt his heart quicken. At last. He was almost there, but he suddenly felt homesick. He missed his grandmother and his brother, and yes, he even missed his dad. Glen was a virtual stranger, but Santiago couldn't wait to see him.

The train cruised back to high speed, and as Santiago glanced from the window to his right, he saw the magnificent metal sculpture *The Angel of the North,* standing proudly beyond the hill running up from the trackside.

He couldn't judge how far away it was, but even from this distance it was stunning. Arms, or wings, outstretched, it reminded Santiago of a joyous soccer player celebrating a Cup-winning goal. In less than half a minute, *The Angel* had disappeared behind trees, but the image stayed with Santiago until the train began to slow down.

To the right of the train, rows of terraced houses ran uphill, and away to his left, as the winter sky darkened, the young Latin American got his first sight of the sprawling city.

"The next stop will be Newcastle," said the voice on the PA. "Newcastle, next stop."

The rhythmic sound of the wheels on the tracks changed suddenly as the train rumbled slowly across the River Tyne. Santiago saw another bridge to his left and to his right he counted four, no, five, more bridges.

The sound of the wheels changed again and the train slid smoothly into the cavern of Newcastle Central Station.

Santiago pulled down his bag and followed the other passengers down onto platform four. He walked through a short tunnel, just as Glen had told him, and then up a ramp to cross to the main concourse.

Glen was waiting, exactly as he had said he would be. "It's great to see you, son," he said, grabbing Santiago's bag. "But why didn't you call me from the States to let me know you were coming?"

"I had to wait in Mexico for my passport. I only got it yesterday." They were walking to the main exit. "It's not okay that I'm here?"

"No, it's fine; you caught me a bit off guard, that's all. You can stay with me till you get sorted."

At the main exit, a long line of taxis stood waiting for passengers ready to be whisked off to various parts of the city. But Glen motioned to the left and they kept walking. "Welcome to The Toon."

"The Toon? What is The Toon?"

"This place. Where the Geordies live."

Santiago was struggling to keep up with the conversation. "What is a Geordie?"

Glen smiled. "Someone who lives in The Toon. You've got a lot to learn, bonny lad."

Glen lived at Tynemouth, in a neat semidetached house on the promenade opposite the sands and the North Sea. He parked his Audi in the driveway next to the well-kept front garden and they both got out of the car.

Santiago shivered as the bitterly cold north wind blew in from the sea. It was almost dark now, but he could just make out the gray water and angry white waves breaking on the shoreline. It sure didn't look like the Pacific over there.

Glen smiled as he took in Santiago's light, L.A.-style clothes. "You're not exactly dressed for these parts."

"I didn't realize it would be so cold."

"Cold? This is what we call bracing. You wait till the weather turns bad! Come on, let's get you inside."

The house was as well kept as the garden but seemed, to Santiago, neat and functional rather than lived-in and warm as he had imagined.

"You live here alone?"

Glen nodded. "My wife died three years ago."

"I'm sorry."

"I miss her," said Glen with a sigh. "This place has never felt the same. That's why it was good to see my daughter out in your part of the world. I've got a son, too, but he lives in London and he's just got engaged, so I don't see him very often."

Santiago unzipped his bag, took out a small statue, and handed it to Glen.

"It is the Virgin of Guadalupe. My grandmother had this since she was a little girl, but she wanted you to have it. It will bring blessings on your house."

"I'm very touched, Santiago," said Glen, looking a little embarrassed. "I'm not a very good Catholic, mind."

"But my grandmother thinks you are a good man, and my grandmother is always right."

Glen really was embarrassed now. "Come on, I'll show you your room, and while you're getting settled in, I'll get us some food. I'd better warn you though, I'm no Jamie Oliver."

"Jamie who?"

"Never mind," grinned Glen. "We'll get used to each other."

Glen decided to play it safe on the cooking front. He pulled two frozen shepherd's pies from the freezer and while they were heating in the oven he boiled some water for the accompanying frozen peas.

For the first time in a very long while he laid two places at the kitchen table, and when the food was ready he went to the stairs and called up to Santiago. "Grub's up. D'you fancy a beer?"

There was no reply.

"Santiago?"

There was still no answer. Glen climbed the stairs and knocked gently on the bedroom door. *Still* no answer.

He pushed open the door and saw Santiago sprawled out on the bed, sound asleep. On the bedside table stood a framed photograph of the Muñez family. It looked as though it had been taken three or four years earlier; Glen recognized Mercedes and the younger Santiago and Julio. The two boys were standing on either side of a man Glen guessed must be their father, Herman. He had his arms around his sons' shoulders and looked every bit the proud dad.

Glen tiptoed in, pulled a duvet over his sleeping guest, went back to the door, and switched off the light. "You wouldn't have fancied my shepherd's pie, anyway," he whispered as he closed the door.

9

Santiago was standing by the front door, looking out toward the bleak, gray, forbidding North Sea, when Glen came down the following morning.

"Sleep all right?"

"I woke up early. I'm sorry about the food."

"You didn't miss much. You can grab some breakfast when we get to the workshop."

"Workshop?"

"The place where I work."

"But I thought you worked in football."

Glen smiled. "Not anymore, lad. But don't let that worry you. Come on, I like to get in early."

They drove through quiet streets as the city and suburbs eased into another day. The area around Foy Motors was run-down: rows of terraced houses, many of them boarded up and awaiting the bulldozers.

As they stepped from the Audi, Santiago saw the Foy Motors sign above the roll-up shutters.

"You fix cars?"

Glen unlocked the heavy padlock and pulled up the shutter. "I restore old ones, give them a second lease on life. There's a café just down the road; my lads usually get in there for breakfast before they start work. You get yourself something to eat and we'll go to the club at about ten."

The café was easy enough to find. It was filled with workingmen sitting in clouds of blue cigarette smoke as they downed huge mugs of tea and fried breakfasts, and exchanged early morning banter.

Santiago had no idea what to order, so when he saw the handwritten sign on the wall behind the counter offering "Full Breakfast," he went for that. He sat alone at one of the few vacant tables, and ten minutes later a plate overflowing with bacon, sausages, eggs, beans, tomatoes, and a foul-looking circle of something black with white flecks was placed in front of him.

He picked up his knife and fork, uncertain where to begin, then prodded the black stuff a couple of times to make certain that it wasn't still alive.

At the next table, three men wearing overalls with FOY MOTORS emblazoned on the back were talking soccer; everyone in the place seemed to be talking soccer.

The biggest and loudest of the three was sounding off about Newcastle's latest signing. "I've heard that some of the players have a real problem with Harris. Don't like his attitude."

"Not surprising, is it, Foghorn," said the second man. "Three clubs in five years should tell you something."

The third man, older than the others, nodded wisely. "He's better when he stays inside. If he's not in the mood he drifts out wide and gets lost."

"Maybe he should stay lost," said the aptly named Foghorn, who looked up from his breakfast and saw Santiago staring at him. "What are you looking at?"

Santiago had been trying to understand the strange accents. "I'm sorry, but you talk about football, yes?"

"There's nowt else *to* talk about."

The older man was equally intrigued by Santiago's accent. "Where you from, son?"

"Los Angeles."

Foghorn was suddenly interested. "Oh, aye? D'you know Charlize Theron? She's a cracker."

Santiago grinned. "Oh sure, she's over at my place all the time."

The throwaway line went down well with the Geordies.

"You're a long way from home," said the older one. "What you doing up here?"

"I have a tryout for Newcastle United."

"A trial!" Foghorn's voice boomed through the café. "Howay! I had one, you know. They offered me fifty grand a week and a house by a golf course. But I said no, I prefer being a paint sprayer. Isn't that right, Walter?"

Walter was the older man. "Paint spraying's all you're good for, Foghorn." He turned back to Santiago. "Are you serious, lad?"

"Yes. Maybe today. Your boss, Glen, arranged it for me."

"Did he now? He kept that quiet."

"Aye, he did," said Foghorn, leaning toward Santiago. "If you're having a trial today, you'll need to run like a whippet." He speared the black blob on Santiago's plate with his fork and transferred it to his own. "You'd better give this black pudding a miss."

Glen's car was behind a double-decker bus. It was all so strange to Santiago. The leaden sky, the gray city streets, everyone in heavy winter clothes. Nothing was familiar or reassuring.

The traffic moved slowly, held in a succession of traffic lights, as Glen edged the Audi through the busy, bustling city.

"What you have to understand, Santiago, is that football's a religion in these parts. In London, you've got any number of clubs, same in the Midlands. There's two in Manchester and two in Liverpool. But up here, it's just The Toon."

After his conversation in the café and Glen's explanation, Santiago was beginning to understand the almost fanatical devotion of the Newcastle United supporters. "You don't speak like people from The Toon."

"I'm Irish. Came over to play thirty years ago and never left."

"Why?"

"I like it here." The car was moving slightly uphill. They reached a traffic circle, and as Glen moved the vehicle away again he nodded to Santiago to look up ahead. "There she is."

Santiago's eyes widened and his mouth gaped. Directly ahead was St. James' Park. It dominated the skyline. Glen had said soccer was like a religion in these parts, and St. James' Park stood there like a massive, modern cathedral: a towering structure of concrete, glass, and metal.

"Not bad, eh?"

Santiago couldn't answer. He just stared.

Glen parked the car and they walked back to the stadium and down a driveway, which slid beneath part of the huge arena.

On the outer side of the high-roofed tunnel, elevators and escalators soared away toward the administration and hospitality areas of the stadium. Midway along the inner side were steps leading to double glass doors. The sign above the doors read: PLAYERS AND OFFICIALS ENTRANCE.

"We timed it right," said Glen. "There's the man himself."

Erik Dornhelm, dressed in an expensive suit and looking more like a high-powered executive than a soccer team manager, was standing on the steps, deep in conversation with another man. Glen took Santiago's arm and gestured that they should wait. As soon as the conversation ended, he urged his young friend forward and called to Dornhelm before he could continue up the steps.

"Morning, Mr. Dornhelm. This is the young man I was telling you about. Santiago Muñez. From Los Angeles."

Dornhelm showed no sign of remembering the late-night conversation. "When was this?"

"When I called you in the middle of the night and you promised to give him a tryout."

"I did?"

The throaty roar of a serious sports car engine echoed through the tunnel, and all three men turned to see an Aston Martin convertible pull to a standstill. Gavin Harris emerged from the driver's seat, cell phone at one ear.

"One moment, please," said Dornhelm to Glen and he walked over to Harris, who instantly terminated his phone call.

"Morning, boss," he said with a smile.

Dornhelm was in no mood for exchanging pleasantries, and Glen and Santiago heard every word exchanged between the Newcastle manager and his new midfielder. "I'm sure you have a watch, and I'm sure it's a Rolex. What time does it say?"

Gavin didn't bother checking his Rolex. "Yeah, sorry, boss. I called in at the hospital; dropped off a shirt for a sick kid. We should have had the PR people there—would have made a great photo."

Dornhelm remained stony-faced. "Gavin, this is bullshit. We have six journalists inside waiting to interview you; they have been waiting for fifty minutes. Get in there! And when you've finished with the press, you train with the reserves!"

Gavin knew better than to argue. He just nodded and hurried up the steps. Dornhelm returned to Santiago and Glen. "Where were we?"

"I called you," said Glen. "About Santiago here."

Dornhelm almost smiled. "Yes, my wife remembers it well." He looked at Santiago. "Where do you play?"

"In Los Angeles," said Santiago nervously.

"I mean, in which position do you play?"

"Oh. For my team I play up front. But I prefer midfield. That way I get to see more of the ball."

Dornhelm studied Santiago for a few moments, appearing to size him up, and then nodded to Glen. "Get him over to the training ground. Let's see what he's got."

He walked up the steps and disappeared into the building through the glass doors. Santiago looked at Glen. "My trial? It isn't here?"

Glen smiled. "No, lad, you'll have to wait a bit longer before you make your first appearance at St. James'."

The training complex had been recently refurbished. A dozen soccer fields clustered around a converted manor house with state-of-the-art training facilities, treatment and changing rooms, a restaurant, and offices.

Santiago sat alone on a bench in the vast changing room. He was wearing training gear he'd been given and a brand-new pair of soccer cleats. He tied the laces and thought to himself that a pair of shoes like these would have cost him a month's wages back home.

He was nervous. He stood up and reached into his jacket pocket for his asthma inhaler. He took a quick puff and slipped it back into his pocket just as a track-suited man of around Glen's age walked into the room.

"All set?"

Santiago nodded.

The new arrival held out his hand. "I'm Mal Braithwaite, first-team coach."

They shook hands and Santiago tried to look a lot more confident than he felt. Braithwaite wasn't fooled. "Glen's told me all about you. We go back a long way, so I'm on your side."

"Thank you, sir."

"I'm not a 'sir.' I'm 'Coach.' 'Sir' is the gaffer and he's checking you out today."

He saw Santiago's bewildered look and smiled. "You ready?"

"Yes, si— Coach, I'm ready."

He followed Braithwaite from the changing room, crossing himself as he went.

Rain was falling steadily as they emerged into the gloom of the bleak winter's day. It wasn't what Santiago was expecting and certainly not what he'd been praying for as he crossed himself.

On a field nearby, two teams wearing colored bibs were playing a practice match. Glen stood watching, his coat collar up around his neck. He winked at Santiago as Braithwaite whistled to one of the players to come off the field.

The game stopped for a moment as Braithwaite put an arm on one of Santiago's shoulders and pointed toward Gavin Harris, who was looking far from happy out on one wing.

"Midfield, on the right. Slot inside Gavin."

Santiago pulled a bib over his head and jogged onto the field. The other players watched curiously as he moved alongside Gavin Harris, who totally ignored Santiago's nervous smile.

Close to the touchline, a big central defender wandered toward Braithwaite. "Who's this, then?"

"Young Mexican lad. Be gentle with him, Hughie."

"Oh, you know me, Coach, I'll be as gentle as a lamb."

Hughie Magowan was six feet two and tough as teak. He reveled in his hard man reputation and thought of every one of his numerous yellow cards as battle honors, campaign medals. He was nearing the end of a long and bruising career, and many Premiership strikers still bore the scars they had collected in their close encounters with Hughie Magowan.

These days Hughie spent most of his time adding experience and steel to the youth and enthusiasm of the reserve team; he only ever got a sniff of the first-team squad in an emergency. He would be little missed when he finally hung up his cleats, but until then Hughie intended to carry on making his mark—literally.

The game resumed, the rain fell steadily, and the ball stubbornly refused to come anywhere near Santiago. He was uncertain as to whether he should go looking for it or hold his position.

Glen watched with growing frustration, and after five minutes Braithwaite called out to a young midfielder, who was playing a deeper, holding role on the same team as Santiago. "Franny! Bring the kid into the game!"

The midfielder nodded and the next time he picked up the ball, he sent a long pass directly into Santiago's path. It wasn't a difficult ball, not for anyone used to British conditions. But as it skidded off the muddy turf, Santiago totally misjudged the bounce and the ball slipped away over the touchline.

Santiago felt as stupid as he had looked and a few of the players raised their eyebrows or exchanged "He's useless" type glances.

Hughie Magowan was a lot more direct. He didn't

mince his words, only opposition players. "Bloody amateur," he growled.

As the ball was recovered, Mal Braithwaite turned to Glen. "Are you sure about him?"

"Give him a chance, Mal," said Glen. "He's not used to these conditions."

The throw-in was taken and Glen saw Erik Dornhelm, now in a tracksuit and looking a lot more comfortable for it, come striding out from the changing rooms.

Carl Francis, the young black player known as Franny to everyone on the Newcastle staff, was doing his best to give Santiago another opportunity. He collected the ball from a defender and sent it, more gently this time, toward the newcomer. The pass could have done with more weight and Santiago was forced to run back toward his own goal to collect it.

An opposing forward came charging toward him and Santiago knew that the safe and obvious option was the simple pass back to his central defender. But he was out to impress. As the forward lumbered in, Santiago feinted to one side, swiveled, and jinked away. The forward was left charging at air.

Mal looked at Glen. "He's a funny one. Awkward one minute and then he does something like that."

Glen smiled and turned toward Erik Dornhelm.

He wasn't watching; he was talking on his cell phone with his back turned from play.

Santiago still had the ball. He moved diagonally across the field and delivered an inch-perfect pass to Gavin Harris. He didn't see what happened next. As Harris went for the shot, Santiago's legs were swept away as Hughie Magowan finally arrived with his late, late tackle.

"Welcome to Newcastle, *amigo,*" grinned Hughie as Santiago picked himself up from the mud.

Gavin's shot had been deflected off a defender for a corner. Santiago jogged into the opposition box, and Franny directed him to a position near the back post. He found some space and, as the ball swung across from the corner flag, he ran and jumped. Hughie was all over him like a rash; this guy could have fouled for England.

The ball went clear and the players swept from the box, leaving Santiago facedown in the mud.

It didn't get much better. There was the occasional inspired touch or flick, but overall Santiago spent more time on his backside than on his feet as Hughie, along with a couple of the other defenders who joined in the fun, completed his introduction to old-fashioned, blood-and-thunder British football.

But every time Santiago went down, he got gamely

to his feet, without complaint and ready for more. It was like nothing he had experienced before, a totally different game from the one he played and dominated back in the California sunshine.

Glen fretted on the touchline, painfully aware that Dornhelm appeared to have seen enough and was getting ready to leave. He was talking on his cell again as he walked slowly along the touchline.

On the field, Santiago ran on to a bouncing ball. He flicked it over one defender's head with a move as skillful as one by Ronaldinho, and as Hughie charged in, he nutmegged the big man, hearing him curse as he sped away. Gavin Harris was lurking near the edge of the box. Santiago played a neat pass and kept running, and unselfishly Gavin turned the pass into a lovely one-two.

Santiago hit the ball on the run, and it curled goalward and rattled the upright. As the ball was scrambled away, the assistant coach who was refereeing whistled for a foul.

Gavin Harris picked up the ball and placed it carefully for the free kick, ready to remind the manager and head coach exactly why the club had forked out £8.4 million for his services.

But it wasn't to be.

"Let the new lad take it!" yelled Mal Braithwaite.

Gavin shrugged and moved aside, in some way curious to see what the youngster would make of the dead ball opportunity.

The defenders formed a wall, Hughie in the middle, as the goalkeeper shouted his instructions.

On the touchline, Glen's thoughts went back to California and the stunning free kick he'd watched Santiago take against the Croatian team. The ball was closer to the goal this time, the angle less acute; it was an easier shot.

"Do it again, Santi," breathed Glen. "Just do it again."

Santiago appeared to have exactly that in mind, setting himself up in a similar way, only a couple of strides from the ball.

The whistle blew, he took the two strides, pulled back his right foot—and felt himself start to slip in the mud. He was completely off balance, and as he slithered backward to the ground, his foot connected with the ball and sliced it high and wide of the goal.

The miss was greeted with the inevitable jeers from the other players and Hughie came running out from the defensive wall, his smile as wide as the mouth of the River Tyne. He leaned down toward Santiago with his arm outstretched as though he was going to help him to his feet. But as Santiago reached upward,

Hughie drew back his arm and turned the outstretched hand of friendship into a dismissive wave of farewell. *"Adios, amigo."*

"All right, that's enough," shouted Mal from the touchline. "Four laps round the perimeter."

The other players set off on their cooldown run, jeering, moaning, and complaining about their slave driver of a coach. Before Santiago could get up and join them, Mal shouted again. "Not you, Santiago. You get yourself down to the showers."

As Santiago struggled up from the mud he saw Mal turn to Glen and shake his head.

They were back at Glen's house. The drive back from the training ground had been awkward, beginning in silence, with neither of them knowing quite what to say.

Santiago, bruised and battered, ran through the whole painful experience again in his mind, and when he came to the humiliating experience of the free kick, he felt himself redden with embarrassment.

"My legs wouldn't do what my brain was telling me," he said at last. "I'll be better tomorrow, I promise. I know I'll be better."

There was no way Glen could let him down gently. "There won't be a tomorrow, Santi. I'm sorry. I argued with Mal, but . . ."

His voice died away. There was nothing more to say. Santiago had been expecting it anyway, but until the words were said, he had clung to the hope that just maybe he had shown enough to be given one more chance.

It was over, almost before it had begun.

Glen felt the disappointment almost as acutely as Santiago. He *knew* what the boy could do; he'd seen that special talent with his own eyes. It was almost criminal to let such a talent go to waste. But what more could he do?

Santiago had been up in the bedroom for a while. Glen stood at the living-room window, watching the day darken and the North Sea remorselessly roll in against the shoreline.

He heard footsteps on the stairs and Santiago appeared at the doorway. "My father believes people have a place in life. You work, you feed your family, you die, and it's foolish to think otherwise."

Glen was still gazing out of the window, watching wave after wave wash onto the sand. "Aye, my old man fed me the same line. Which is why he swept factory floors for his whole life."

"Could I make a phone call please, Glen?"

Glen turned from the window. "What for?"

"To my grandmother. To tell her I'm coming home."

"No."

"But . . . but it won't take long. And I'll pay for the call."

"I mean, don't call her. Not yet. I want to make a call first."

10

IT WAS PART of a manager's job, particularly the manager of a club like Newcastle United.

No club could exist and thrive without the loyalty of its supporters, so getting out there in the community went with the territory. Invitations had to be accepted to various school and hospital visits, meetings with local businessmen, charity events and black-tie dinners.

At some functions, it was enough just to be there, to be seen, to shake hands and pass on a little tidbit of information about the club that the listeners thought they alone were hearing. Of course, they never were.

On other, more formal occasions, there were speeches to be made, and while Erik Dornhelm was not a natural at public speaking, he took his responsibility seriously and always arrived with a few well-prepared words. His approach was simple: Open with a little laugh—nothing sidesplitting; Dornhelm was no comedian—then get to the point and end with another soccer joke. Above all, keep it brief and don't bore them rigid.

Tonight was one of those occasions, the Northern Merit Awards. Two hundred people—the men in black tie, the women in evening dress—were gathered together in the splendid reception room of the Gosforth Park Hotel.

They were seated in groups of twelve at round tables heavy with gleaming silver and sparkling glassware.

Dornhelm was doing his best to appear completely interested as the wife of a local garage owner told him how her late father had once been a stalwart for Accrington Stanley and would undoubtedly have gone on to play for England if only the Second World War hadn't intervened.

"Of course, by the time it was over he was too old. Sad, isn't it?"

"Yes, very sad," said Dornhelm, thinking that it was about time the main course arrived.

He looked up and saw someone heading for the table. But it wasn't a waiter. It was Glen Foy.

"Sorry to interrupt proceedings but at least I got here before the speeches."

Dornhelm sighed with irritation. "I am making one of those speeches, Mr. Foy. This distraction is not welcome."

"Yeah, well, I wouldn't be here if you answered my calls."

The other guests at the table had ended their own conversations; this was far more interesting.

"What do you want, Mr. Foy?"

"Santiago, the kid. What happened today wasn't fair. The boy grew up in poverty and hardship; his only way out is his skill with the ball."

Dornhelm picked up his wineglass and took a sip as Glen continued.

"He comes to England on my say-so, travels six thousand miles, he's got jet lag, he's nervous, and you put him on a muddy pitch in borrowed boots and then you spend most of your time on your mobile. It's not fair. It's not right."

As Dornhelm glanced to his left, he saw that the woman he'd been speaking to was now staring at him reproachfully and shaking her head as though she agreed with every word Glen had spoken.

Dornhelm coughed. "Your discovery seemed to be flat on his ar—" He looked toward the woman next to him. "Flat on his back for most of the time."

"There was one magic moment," said Glen quickly. "He took the ball on the bounce and—"

"I saw it!" said Dornhelm more loudly than he had intended.

Two waiters arrived and began serving the main course from silver platters.

Glen smiled at a woman seated across the table. "Looks good. I've already eaten, but I'm told they do you very well here." He looked back at Dornhelm. "Listen, I know what I'm talking about. I was a scout, remember? And a good one. And I remember muddy days, watching young lads clogging each other all over the park. But just once in a while, you'd see one who'd lift your heart. Like this lad. Give him a month? That's all I'm asking. One month?"

Glen held his arms out from his sides, palms upward, as though he was appealing to the other diners around the table for their support. He didn't need to; it had been quite a performance.

Dornhelm was aware that everyone, even his own wife, was staring at him, silently urging him to answer the right way. He picked up his wineglass and took a sip.

Off the living room at Glen Foy's house was a small alcove. It was like a shrine to soccer, and to Glen's career.

After Glen went out, saying he "had a little business to do," Santiago watched television for a while, but soon grew tired of the endless reality programs. He'd had enough reality for one day. He left the set switched on and went into the alcove, where for the first time since his arrival he took the time to study the framed photographs closely.

The young Glen was easy to spot in the Newcastle United and Irish international team lineups. There were more photos: Glen in different teams, Glen the tracksuited manager.

Santiago picked up a scrapbook and was soon engrossed. Black-and-white photographs, match programs, faded newspaper clippings. Santiago read every word and smiled each time he came to a mention of his friend.

The television was blaring out the theme tune to another program and Santiago didn't hear the car pull up outside or Glen enter the house.

"That was all a long time ago."

Santiago jumped as he looked up and saw Glen leaning against the wall. "I'm sorry, I was just—"

"No problem. My wife did all that. I never got round to clearing it away."

"You never told me you were major league."

Glen smiled. "Not for long enough, though. I did my knee in." He picked up a photograph of a Newcastle team from the late 1970s. "Look at that. Shorts were shorter and hair was longer, and we didn't drive Aston Martins or Ferraris."

"But you were still heroes."

"Oh, yeah. Footballers have always been heroes, even in my father's day when they made eight quid a week and worked down the mine. Working people have always needed their football. It lifts them; it's something more to think about and talk about than the struggle of day-to-day life."

He replaced the photograph on top of the cabinet. "Go on a bit, don't I? But it's the reason I was so proud to put on the skipper's shirt." As he spoke, he pulled open a drawer in the cabinet and took out a neatly folded Newcastle United shirt. He let it fall loose and Santiago spotted the number six on the back. "Here," said Glen, passing him the shirt.

"I cannot accept this; it is too special," said Santiago, shaking his head.

"I'm not giving it to you, lad! I just want you to try it on, see what you look like in the black and white."

Santiago's face fell. "What's the point now?"

Glen smiled. "The point is, I had another little chat with Erik Dornhelm tonight. I gave him a touch of indigestion, and he's given you a month's trial. So go on, try it on."

11

THE TRAINING-GROUND DRESSING ROOM was crowded with reserve squad players. Most were changed into training gear, the younger ones anxious to get out and impress coaches and management; a few veterans, like Hughie Magowan, more intent on going through the motions and keeping their heads down.

A player like Hughie had nothing to prove. Everyone knew what he could do—or these days what he *couldn't* do. He was still, just about, an asset to the club. In an emergency, he had the know-how and experience to slot into the first team and do a passable job, as long as the opposing strikers didn't have the pace of a Thierry Henry or a Jermain Defoe. And with the reserves, he could give the youngsters a genuine taste of what life would be like for them if and when they made it through to the big time.

But time was against Hughie, and he knew it. And he didn't much fancy the prospect of playing out a last couple of seasons in the basement divisions, or living on the reduced wages such a move would bring.

The dressing-room banter was centered on the recent first-team performances and the fact that Gavin Harris had hardly set Newcastle on fire since his much-heralded arrival. Some of the older guys were mouthing off about his lack of effort and commitment to the team.

"Another glory boy," moaned Hughie. "Only in it for himself. He doesn't give a toss about which club he plays for; it's just the money for blokes like him."

The younger ones listened and wisely kept their mouths shut, more concerned about getting a chance to make their mark before the end of the season and having their contracts renewed.

The door swung open and Mal Braithwaite walked in with a nervous-looking Santiago and the reserve-team coach, Bobby Redfern.

"Listen up, you lot," said Mal. "Say hello to Santiago Muñez."

"I thought we'd already said good-bye to him," said Hughie, not bothering to join in with the general nods of hello and welcome.

Mal completely ignored Hughie's sarcasm. "Santiago's from Mexico."

"I'm from Los Angeles," said Santiago. "I was born in Mexico."

Mal smiled. "Oh, are you? Well, there we are then. Now you all know everything you need to know. And before the day's out I want all of you to let Santiago know exactly who you are."

Hughie finished tying a shoelace and stood up. "It'll be a pleasure, Coach."

Before Mal's "get to know Santiago" instructions could really take place during another practice game, there was a meticulously planned, high-pressure morning of training, starting with a full warm-up, including gentle stretches and aerobic work.

Santiago could hardly believe he was actually there, but the full reality of everything that had happened over the past few days hit him as he glanced across to the adjacent field to see Erik Dornhelm arrive with the first-team squad. He'd seen Gavin Harris before, but now he was getting his first look at the other big names.

He was like a kid in a candy store as his eyes darted from one player to another: Shearer, Given, Jenas, Dyer.

Bobby Redfern saw him staring. "Hey, Muñez! Never mind that lot, get on with what you're meant to be doing!"

The second-stringers went into phase two of training. Fifty-meter sprints, jinking through slalom cones, knee-lift runs through lines of tires, dead ball and passing practice.

Santiago had always thought he was fit, but he had known nothing like this before. The *Americanitos* training nights had usually amounted to little more than a kickaround, with everyone crowded around one goal trying to beat the keeper, followed by a five- or six- or seven-a-side match, depending on how many players had bothered to turn up.

By the time the practice match started, Santiago was tired, but he wasn't going to let anyone else know that. And the introductions Mal had spoken of might have been a pleasure for the others, but the new boy found them far from pleasurable.

Hughie Magowan was particularly "welcoming." His crunching tackles were meant to leave their mark. And they did. But each time Santiago went down he got up and got on with the game without complaint, and by the time Mal whistled for the end of the game, even Hughie was slightly, if reluctantly, impressed.

It was a long, hard first session, and when it was over Santiago only had time to shower and change before being whisked off for a full medical examination.

He was given a white hospital robe, a form on a clipboard, and a clear beaker with his name written on it, then directed to a small room with instructions to get changed, fill in the form, and fill the beaker. Santiago was getting used to following orders and a few minutes later he walked into the examination room holding the clipboard and his filled beaker in one hand, while the other clutched at the back of the hospital robe to prevent it from coming apart.

A young and very attractive nurse with dark hair pinned back was sitting at a desk, filling in a form. She looked up as Santiago entered.

When he smiled self-consciously at her, she didn't return the smile but simply stood up and took the clipboard and beaker from his outstretched hand.

"Sit there, please," she said, nodding toward the examination table.

Santiago perched on the edge of the table and the nurse wrapped a strap around his arm as she prepared to take his blood pressure. She began pumping air into the valve but avoided Santiago's eyes as he smiled again.

"It may be a little high," said Santiago.

"Oh. Why's that?"

"I didn't think the club doctor would look so good."

"I'm not the club doctor, I'm the club doctor's nurse." She released the pressure on the valve and the air hissed out. "The club doctor will be along to examine you soon."

The nurse was obviously unimpressed by players' pickup lines. She made a note of the blood pressure reading. "Did you fill in the paperwork?"

"Some words I didn't understand."

The nurse picked up the clipboard and moved back to Santiago. "Like what?"

"This one," said Santiago, pointing at the form.

"Cardiovascular. It means heart problems."

Santiago smiled. "No, no." He pointed at another word. "And this one?"

"Respiratory. Do you have problems with your lungs, or breathing?"

Santiago hesitated. Of course he did. He had asthma. But he wasn't going to let that get in the way of his entire future. It wasn't a problem. It never had been.

"Well?" said the nurse.

"No, no way."

"Fine. Step against the wall, please. I need to make a note of your height."

Santiago moved across to the measure on the wall, and the nurse had to stand very close as she took the reading.

"What's your name?" asked Santiago.

"Harmison," said the nurse, showing Santiago her laminated name badge. "*Nurse* Harmison."

"I mean, your first name?"

"You don't need to know that. You don't need to know where I live, or my phone number, what my star sign is, or what I'm doing on Saturday night. Now, sit on the chair, please. I have to take some blood."

Santiago sighed and sat on the chair. "Oh, man, I don't like those things," he said as *Nurse* Harmison advanced with the needle raised.

"But you've got a tattoo," said the nurse as she saw the Aztec symbol on his arm. "Or is it just a rub-on transfer?"

"That was a gang thing," said Santiago with a shrug.

"A gang? You were in a gang?"

"I'm from east L.A., I had no choice. And once you're in, there's only three ways to get out. You get shot, you go to jail, or you're like me, you have a grandmother who kicks some sense into you."

The young nurse looked hard at Santiago, and for a moment she almost smiled. Then she raised her eyebrows and went back to looking at the needle. Slowly and carefully, she eased it into Santiago's arm.

"Ay-ee!"

"Sorry, tough guy." This time, she did smile. "My name's Roz."

———

That evening, over one of Glen's specialty frozen shepherd's pies, Santiago gave his host a full rundown of what had happened during his first day at the club.

Glen wanted to know the lot; he'd been thinking about his young protégé all day at the garage, hoping that the Newcastle coaches would begin to see the talent he'd spotted during those matches back in California.

"I think it went okay," Santiago told him. "Bobby Redfern didn't say I did good, but he didn't say I did bad, either."

"What about Dornhelm, did he see you?"

"No, he was with the first-team squad all day. I don't think he even knew I was there."

"Oh, he knew all right," said Glen. "And he'll know exactly how you did."

By nine o'clock Santiago was feeling exhausted, his whole body aching after his first full day of training. But before turning in for an early night there was something he wanted to do. "Glen, can I call my grandmother? She will want to know what happened today. I will pay for the call."

"Of course you can call her, lad. Give her my best, and tell her that statue is standing by my bed."

Nine P.M. English time was one P.M. in California. It was a good time to call. Mercedes was sure to be

"No shin pads, no game."

Playing for the *Americanitos,* one chance is usually all Santiago needs.

Santiago's father doesn't share his dream.

Gavin Harris signs for
Newcastle United.

right: On a muddy
field in borrowed
shoes after a journey
of six thousand
miles . . .

The routine of day-to-day training . . .

Santiago doesn't tell the *whole* truth at his medical exam . . .

. . . but ends up struggling for breath with no explanation.

right: Practice makes perfect.

home, while Julio would be at school and Herman at work.

As Santiago spoke in Spanish to Mercedes from the cold, dark corner of northeast England, he could almost see and feel the sunshine of California.

His grandmother's questions about training were almost as detailed as Glen's had been, and when Santiago finally got through his story for a second time, he heard his grandmother laugh contentedly. "We're proud of you, you know that, Santiago, don't you?"

"What about Dad, is he proud of me?"

There was a pause. "You know your father, he doesn't talk about you much."

"And what he does say isn't good, eh?"

Mercedes quickly changed the subject. "Tell me about England. Do you like it? Is the scenery beautiful?"

Santiago thought back to his meeting with Roz Harmison. "Oh, yes, Grandmother, some of the scenery is very beautiful."

12

Santiago slipped into the routine of day-to-day training as easily as he always thought he would. He even began to get accustomed to the biting cold and overcast skies.

Most of the reserve squad was welcoming and Santiago quickly struck up a friendship with another young player, a Liverpudlian by the name of Jamie Drew.

Even the first-teamers were friendly enough when they crossed paths with the second-stringers, in the changing room, or the canteen, or during a combined first team and reserves session in the gymnasium.

The gym was state of the art, with an impressive array of muscle-building and body-strengthening machines and equipment. Santiago had to be taught how to use the machines without injuring himself, but once he knew, he wanted to try the lot.

He was doing leg-lifts, strengthening his calf muscles, with as much weight as he could handle.

His target was fifty. He reached thirty with no problem. Then it got tougher. Each lift got harder, and slower. He got to forty and kept going, counting down the last ten in Spanish. Sweat stood out on his brow, his eyes closed tightly to aid his concentration. Forty-five. He paused for a second and then went on. Just five more. He had to do it. Forty-six, forty-seven, forty-eight . . . forty-nine. It was agony. Fifty!

Santiago gasped as he let the leg weights sink back into position. He lifted his head and opened his eyes—Alan Shearer stood there watching him.

"Finished with that, son?"

"Oh! Oh, sure. Sorry."

"No problem."

Santiago climbed unsteadily off the machine and watched as Shearer took the seat and began adding more weights. Ten pounds, then another ten, and then another. He began his own exercise, making it look as easy as a stroll in the park.

Santiago, calves aching, went over to Jamie, who was working on another machine.

"Alan Shearer," said Santiago.

"What about him?"

"He spoke to me."

Jamie smiled. "No!"

Everyone seemed to just accept Santiago, and to treat him as though he was part of the club. With one exception—Hughie Magowan.

Hughie made no secret of his dislike for Santiago, with snide comments and jibes every time he was in earshot. By the end of the first week, the constant barrage of criticism and insults was beginning to get to the young Mexican.

The reserve squad was playing another training game when the volatile situation finally came to the boil.

Mal Braithwaite was looking in on the reserves' progress and was trying out different playing formations. He'd put Santiago up front, playing in the lone striker's role.

Santiago wasn't particularly happy about it. As always, he would have preferred his favored attacking midfield position, but he was getting on with the job, even though he was seeing far less of the ball than he would have liked.

He'd already taken a couple of hefty knocks from big Hughie, and with the frustration of playing out of position and only a few weeks to impress, he could feel his temper starting to rise.

Then, from a high clearance from the opposing keeper, one of Santiago's teammates headed the ball back. It was a chance. As Santiago controlled the ball and turned toward the goal, Hughie came charging in. The two-footed sliding tackle was high and brutal, and Santiago was sent sprawling onto the hard ground.

Even some of Hughie's own team winced and shouted their disapproval.

"Hughie!"

"Not necessary, mate!"

Magowan got up, looking the picture of innocence as Santiago leaped to his feet and went eyeball to eyeball with the big defender. "What's your problem!"

Hughie was well used to situations like this. He stood still, arms at his side, waiting and willing the youngster to take a swing at him. He grinned. "Problem? What problem?"

Mal Braithwaite shouted from the touchline, "Okay, break it up! Walk away!"

The last thing Santiago wanted to do was walk away. He wanted to smash the grinning, taunting face just inches from his. But he didn't. He took a deep breath and turned away. As Hughie jogged back into position Jamie Drew walked up to Santiago. "Forget it, he's not worth it."

Santiago nodded and rubbed his bruised leg. But

the incident soured the rest of the game and he didn't perform well.

He was still seething after he'd showered and changed and was standing in the canteen, lining up for lunch with Jamie.

"Look, forget about it," said Jamie, seeing Santiago's still clouded face. "There are plenty of Hughie Magowans around."

"Yeah, I guess you're right."

"I know I am. And you don't have time for carrying grudges."

"You're definitely right about that," said Santiago as he began helping himself to food.

"How long did they give you?"

"A month."

"A month! At least I got six. I was at Notts County before this. They signed me from school."

"And how's it going?"

Jamie shrugged. "Early days. Too soon to tell."

They found an empty table and, as they began to eat, some of the first-team players came in and joined the line. Gavin Harris was among them, but he seemed a lot more interested in the phone conversation he was having on his cell than in anything at the buffet.

"Gavin Harris," said Jamie, nodding toward the new arrival. "They paid more than eight million for him."

"Yeah, I know, and he plays in my position. He'd better watch his back, huh?"

Jamie smiled, but his face changed as he saw Hughie Magowan walking toward their table with his own lunch tray. He stopped and looked down at the pasta Santiago had chosen and raised his eyebrows. "No burritos on the menu today? I'll speak to the manager, see if they can get some in special." Before Santiago could reply, Hughie went on, "No thanks, I won't join you. You enjoy your meal; you won't be having many more here, will you?"

Magowan walked on and found a table of his own.

"After the tackle he made on you today, he's the one who shouldn't be here," said Jamie.

Santiago put his fork down by the side of his plate. He had suddenly lost his appetite. "But he could be right. I don't have long to convince them that I'm worth keeping on."

Jamie shrugged and dug into his own bowl of pasta. "Then you'd better have a good look at Newcastle while you've still got a chance."

"What?"

"I could show you the town tonight. Go clubbing, if you like."

Santiago thought for a moment. Since his arrival in England he'd spent every night with Glen, and much as he liked him, he realized he could do with a night out with people his own age. "Sure. Do I need ID?"

"ID? What for?"

"How old do you have to be here to get a drink?"

Jamie smiled through a mouthful of pasta. "Eleven."

Santiago found it hard to shake off the memory of Hughie Magowan's ferocious tackle, and even harder to forget his comment in the canteen.

Training was over for the day, so Santiago went back to the house. Glen was already there, having finished work early. He was in the kitchen making himself a cup of tea when he heard the door open. Santiago came in, dropped his bag on the floor, and slumped into an armchair.

"How was it?" called Glen.

Santiago didn't answer.

"Not good?"

"I have a problem with one guy."

The kettle boiled and Glen poured the boiling water into the teapot. He walked through to the living room. "Don't tell me: Hughie Magowan?"

"You know him?"

"Oh, I know him, all right, but fortunately we never met in action."

"He doesn't like me."

"Yeah, well, I can understand that."

"What? But why? I haven't done anything to him."

Glen sat in the chair facing Santiago. "Hughie Magowan is thirty-three; all he's got left is his reputation, and unless every other center back breaks their leg, he'll never play for the first team again."

"That's not my problem."

"No. But you're young, you've got it all in front of you. And on top of that, you've got something Hughie never had. Flair."

Santiago looked puzzled. "I don't know this word."

"It's something most mortals don't have. Most players, myself included, they play within themselves, to their strengths, they don't expose their weaknesses. But the great players, the ones with true flair, they take risks, because they don't believe they are risks. They control the ball; the ball doesn't control them."

"And you think I have this . . . this flair?"

"I know you do, lad. So don't let the Hughie Magowans of this world grind it out of you." He stood up. "Now, d'you fancy a nice cuppa tea?"

13

Santiago had thought Newcastle quayside looked great in the daylight, but at night, as the lights bounced off the Tyne, it was stunning.

From the Tyne Bridge down to the new Gateshead Millennium Bridge, arcing across the river to the Baltic Gallery, the quayside was ablaze with light and buzzing with activity as hundreds of young people moved noisily toward bars and restaurants or spilled out onto the walkways with drinks in their hands.

The cold night didn't appear to have the slightest effect on the dress code of most of the revelers: Blokes were parading in jeans and T-shirts and young women were strutting along in high heels, minuscule skirts, and halter tops.

Santiago was wearing a jacket, done up. He might

have acclimatized himself to the cold of the daytime, but the nights were something else.

He watched two girls in tiny miniskirts with bare legs click their way along the pavement toward a bar and shook his head. "They don't feel cold? It's impossible not to feel cold dressed like that."

"They don't seem to notice it up here," said Jamie. "Must be down to all that Newcastle Brown they drink."

A Range Rover slid past them and came to a halt outside the Club Tabu, where two burly, dark-suited bouncers stood guarding the entrance.

All four doors of the Range Rover sprang open and Gavin Harris emerged from one of the rear doors with two girls. Two guys climbed out of the front. They didn't look like soccer players. One was a good few pounds overweight and the other was as thin as a stick insect. But they acted and sounded as though they were Gavin's best friends as the bouncers welcomed them all to the Club Tabu, especially the soccer player. Celebrities were always welcomed; they were good for business, even if they brought with them a bunch of celebrity hangers-on.

Jamie nudged Santiago. "Come on, we might get in here." He ran toward the club. "Gavin! Hey, Gavin!"

But Gavin and the two girls had already disappeared through the doorway. The larger of Gavin's friends had heard Jamie shout. He turned round. "Write to the club if you want an autograph. Tell 'em Bluto told you to write in."

"You cheeky sod!" said Jamie. "I'm with the club, too!"

Bluto smiled to his friend. "They all say that, don't they, Des?"

"There's always one who tries it on," said Des to the bouncers. "Come on, Bluto, we're missing the action."

As Gavin's friends made their way into the Club Tabu, one of the bouncers replaced the twisted velvet rope across the entrance door, barring the way to Jamie and Santiago.

"I *am* with the club," said Jamie to the two stony-faced bouncers.

"We both are," added Santiago.

"I've never seen you at St. James'," said one of the bouncers.

"We haven't played there yet. We're with the reserves."

The bouncers exchanged a look, uncertain as to whether or not reserves counted as celebrities, even minor celebrities. These guys were paid not only to keep the wrong people out, but also to allow the right people in, and the management didn't look kindly on mistakes.

"What d'you reckon?" said one of the heavies to the other.

They appeared to be hovering on the side of letting Santiago and Jamie in, when Santiago saw a face he recognized on the other side of the road. "Hey, Nurse Harmison!"

Roz Harmison was on a night out with her friend Lorraine. She stopped and stared, quickly recognizing Santiago. "Oh, hello."

"You want to come in this club with us?"

"No way, that place is full of posers."

"So where are you going?"

Roz hesitated, but her friend Lorraine was a lot more forthcoming. "We're going to the Spyglass. You can come with us if you want!"

"*Lorraine!*" said Roz. "This was meant to be a girls' night out."

Her friend smiled. "Don't worry, they look harmless enough." She turned back to Santiago and Jamie. "Well, are you coming or not?"

The Spyglass was a pub more than a club. But it was tastefully decorated, with comfortable chairs and big wooden tables. Best of all, from Santiago's point of view, it had a fire. The logs may have been imitation, but the heat thrown out was real enough.

They found a table close by and sat down with glasses of wine. Eventually Santiago felt warm enough to undo his jacket.

Roz smiled. "Still getting used to our weather?"

"It's not quite like L.A."

Lorraine was sipping her Rioja wine. "L.A.? You're a long way from home."

"Me, too," said Jamie. "I'm from Liverpool."

"Los Angeles and Liverpool. What are you two doing here, then?"

"We play for Newcastle."

Lorraine didn't hide her surprise as she turned to Roz. "I thought you'd put players off-limits."

Roz took a sip of her drink. "They're only trainees."

"Oh, you're in with a chance, then," said Lorraine to Santiago. "Just as long as you don't become a superstar."

Santiago was totally baffled. "I'm sorry, I don't know what this means."

"It means, don't change," said Roz. "Don't become something you're not."

"Oh, I see. At least, I think I see."

Roz laughed. "I remember you now," she said to Jamie. "How's your toe?"

Jamie's eyes widened in horror. He didn't want to go where Roz was going.

"Your big toe," she continued. "Right foot. You had fungus behind the nail."

As Lorraine grimaced and almost choked on her Rioja, a highly embarrassed Jamie smiled a sickly smile at Roz. "Thanks. She's bound to fancy me now, isn't she?"

14

IT WAS RAINING. Hard. Santiago looked out through the windows of the reception area at the training ground and saw many of the first-team squad arrive for the day's training in their Ferraris and Porsches, the sort of cars he had only got close to in L.A. when he was cutting the lawn or clearing the drive for their owners.

He was thinking about what Roz had said in the pub. *Don't change. Don't become something you're not.*

Why would he change? All he wanted to do was to play soccer. To make his living doing something he truly loved. The only way that would change him would be to make him completely happy and fulfilled.

Santiago was already in his training gear. As he

turned away from the window, he saw an Aston Martin come hurtling into the parking lot and skid to a halt on the slippery pavement. Gavin Harris leaped from the driver's seat and ran for the shelter of the building. He was late. Again.

The coaching staff had decided that training would be indoors today. Santiago sat around for a while, waiting for the day to be rescheduled. Eventually Bobby Redfern told him to get down to the indoor playing field.

He'd never seen the Astroturf field until now, and as he walked through the double doors he was amazed at the size of the place. It was enormous, like a hangar for jumbo jets.

Players were already out there, some warming up with easy stretches or slow jogs back and forth across the width of the field, others raining shots at the goalkeeper at the far end. Santiago stared again; the goalkeeper at the far end was Shay Given. And as Santiago's eyes scanned the indoor arena he saw that most of the first-team squad was out there.

Mal Braithwaite was standing on the sideline. He saw Santiago's inquiring look directed at him. "The first team needs a good workout before the Bolton game. Play with the reds. Midfield. Get yourself a bib and do your best."

Santiago grabbed a red bib from the pile and ran onto the field, too nervous to join in any of the warm-ups going on around him.

As Mal prepared to whistle for the start of the game, the double doors opened and Erik Dornhelm walked in.

The first few minutes passed Santiago by as though he wasn't there. Even in a training match, the big boys played at a different pace and Santiago was anxiously trying to adjust to the speed and the unfamiliar playing surface.

Mal jogged by him, his eyes on the game. "C'mon, son, put yourself about."

It was the wake-up call Santiago needed. He went hunting for the ball, and after a few neat touches, he felt his confidence begin to grow.

Gavin Harris received a pass out wide in his own half. He was looking to off-load the ball without too much effort when Santiago nipped in and took it off his toes. Gavin didn't like it, not one bit, and as Santiago moved away, he gave chase, edging Santiago toward the touchline.

The young Latino stopped dead and Harris hesitated, waiting for that split second to make his challenge. But before he could move, Santiago feinted to the left and then did a Ronaldo-like shuffle and went round his right side. He was gone.

On the touchline, Erik Dornhelm caught his chief coach's eye and raised his eyebrows in appreciation.

Santiago was moving at a brisk pace. His strikers were lurking, calling for the ball, perfectly positioned for the well-timed pass. But Santiago had Glen's words at the front of his mind. Risk. Flair.

He had those qualities: Glen had told him so. An opposing midfielder attempted a tackle but Santiago beat him easily. With a defender closing in, Santiago looked up. Risk. Flair.

He let fly with a scorching, rising shot. Shay Given flung himself, full stretch, to his left, and just managed to push the ball round the upright.

Santiago frowned. Close, so close, but not quite close enough. As he jogged back into position he saw Gavin Harris glaring at him.

The electrifying run was Santiago's best moment of the game, but by the time Mal whistled for the end he thought he'd given a reasonable enough account of himself.

As the two teams started to pull off their bibs and make for the doors, Erik Dornhelm picked up a football and walked along the halfway line. "Muñez!"

Santiago ran over to the manager and the other players slowed their departure, curious to see what would happen next.

"When I say 'Go,' I want you to run as fast as you can to the goal."

Some of the older players smiled in anticipation of what was to come.

"Go!"

Santiago turned and sprinted. After a few paces, Dornhelm dropped the ball and volleyed it hard. It flew over Santiago's head, and as he ran he saw it bounce a couple of times and go into the empty net.

"Bring it back to me!" shouted Dornhelm, his voice echoing off the high walls.

The young player scooped the ball from the back of the net and jogged back to the manager.

Dornhelm took the ball and volleyed it again.

"Bring it back to me!"

This time Santiago ran a lot slower as he watched the ball go into the net again. He picked it up and jogged back.

"What did you learn?" said Dornhelm.

"That you can score from halfway?"

Dornhelm was unimpressed by Santiago's reply. "That the ball can travel faster than you can. In my teams, we pass the ball. We play as a unit. I'm not interested in one-man shows."

Gavin Harris was standing nearby and he didn't fail to notice the quick look in his direction as Dornhelm completed his rebuke. "The badge on the front of the shirt is more important than the one on the back."

The words were stinging, humiliating, and as Santiago showered and changed he felt as though the other players were laughing at him. He avoided eye contact with anyone and as he buttoned his shirt he felt the tension in his chest.

There were voices coming from the treatment room and more from the showers, but as he quickly glanced around, he saw that at that moment he was alone.

He reached into his bag, pulled out his asthma inhaler, and took a quick hit.

He didn't see Hughie Magowan walk in from the showers and watch him do it.

15

THERE WAS ALWAYS a huge sense of anticipation at St. James' Park on match days, no matter how the team was performing. If the lads were doing well, their devoted followers turned up expecting another victory. If they were in a bad run, the fans arrived convinced that this was the match in which their heroes' fortunes would change.

From every direction, black-and-white-clad supporters streamed through the city toward the mighty stadium.

As the terraces filled, most of the chatter focused on one topic: that tantalizing finish in the top four of the Premiership which would mean Champions League soccer next season. It was still a possibility, but only just.

The team's recent performances had been stuttering, at best, and with Sam Allardyce's well-drilled, highly experienced outfit for today's opponents, everyone knew the match would be no walkover.

Erik Dornhelm was under pressure, and he knew it. A fresh crop of niggling injuries among the first-team squad wasn't helping, and today a couple of unfamiliar names had been added to the lineup, including Carl Francis, the young midfielder who had been impressive in the reserves.

Santiago and Glen had something many followers of Newcastle could wait for years to get: tickets for a Premiership match. St. James' was all season ticket, apart from some Cup games. But while he was on the playing staff, for however brief a period that might be, Santiago got the opportunity to at least sample the unique atmosphere of St. James', to see the field he dreamed of running onto, and to cheer on his team like any other supporter. Not only that, he'd managed to wangle a club ticket for Glen, too.

As they emerged from one of the access tunnels into the stadium, Santiago stopped and gasped. Nothing he had seen so far in his short time at the club compared with this. The training ground, the indoor facilities, even the exterior of the stadium were amazing, but this . . . this was overwhelming, breathtaking.

Huge stands climbed skyward, filled with a sea of black and white.

"Come on, lad, don't just stand there," said a voice behind Santiago, and he quickly moved on to catch up with Glen.

They found their seats and were flicking through the match program when a voice came over the public address system to give the final lineups. Every one of the home team names was cheered, but at different volume levels, depending on the popularity of each player. The name Alan Shearer, as always, received the loudest cheers.

High up in one of the private boxes, the fact that the name Gavin Harris had received fewer cheers than most didn't go unnoticed by the player's agent, Barry Rankin, or by Gavin's longtime and long-suffering girlfriend, Christina, who had traveled up from London with Barry for the match.

The glass-fronted room was filled to capacity with guests of the star players, all enjoying complimentary prematch drinks and smoked salmon sandwiches. Wolfing down more than most were Gavin's two friends from London, Bluto and Des, who were making the very most of their extended stay on Tyneside.

Barry took Bluto by the arm and spoke quietly so

that his question went unheard by most in the box. "So, is our boy behaving himself?"

"Good as gold," said Bluto through a mouthful of smoked salmon. He saw Christina's doubting look. "Honest!"

There was a roar from the capacity crowd as the players ran onto the field.

"Better take our seats," said Barry, and he ushered Christina out through the open glass doors into the cauldron of St. James' Park.

Erik Dornhelm's face was expressionless as he sat on one of the luxury, heated, airline-type seats in the Newcastle dugout. Beside him, Mal Braithwaite fidgeted nervously and chewed on his nails as Newcastle struggled to gain ascendancy during the first quarter of the match.

A few yards to their left, Sam Allardyce and his Bolton crew were perched on far less comfortable plastic seating in the visitors' dugout. Big Sam didn't appear to care about or even notice the difference in the home and away bench seating arrangements. He was up on his feet every few minutes, bawling instructions to his hardworking team.

The crowd was strangely subdued, perfectly aware that the Newcastle team was not gelling and was far from performing like the unit their manager wanted and demanded. They had enjoyed most of the possession, but it had resulted in not one clear-cut chance on goal.

From his position to the left of and above the dugouts, Santiago could see Mal Braithwaite fretting and could almost sense the unease on the bench. Immediately behind the dugouts, the rows of newspaper and radio journalists were busy with phones and microphones, already putting into words for their readers and listeners what everyone inside the stadium knew was a less than dynamic display by the home team.

And behind the journalists, the chairman, the directors, and their guests shifted uncomfortably in their perfectly comfortable executive chairs.

The first half ended goalless, and as Dornhelm and his players disappeared down the players' tunnel, they left with more than a few jeers from the faithful.

In the stands, Glen was less than impressed. "They're all over the place and Harris isn't in the game."

Santiago was reluctant to criticize his club mates. "Carl Francis is playing well."

"Aye, he looks useful. At least he's trying."

The second half picked up in exactly the same way as the first had ended. Plenty of Newcastle possession, but no end result. Then suddenly there was a chance. Kieron Dyer played a tight through ball into space for Gavin Harris to run on to. But Harris was off the pace and didn't even connect with the ball as he lunged for it.

The crowd groaned and Erik Dornhelm immediately directed two of the Newcastle subs to start warming up.

The Bolton team seemed to take heart from the miss and began enjoying a period of pressure and dominance. Carl Francis intercepted one attack out wide, but as he looked to turn defense into attack he was brought down by a scything tackle.

Francis rolled on the ground, clutching his knee, and as the crowd roared their disapproval, the referee had no hesitation in pulling out the yellow card.

The injury was bad; everyone could tell that by the number of players from both sides who gathered round. Francis was stretchered off to sympathetic applause from the whole crowd and Erik Dornhelm decided then to make not one, but two substitutions.

Up in the executive box, Bluto could hardly believe it. "That cretin is pulling Gavin off! It's ridiculous—he's the only one who's done anything all day!"

Barry Rankin and Christina wisely said nothing.

Close to the end, and against the run of play, Newcastle somehow managed to scramble the ball over the line to take the lead. And in the dying minutes they held on against sustained Bolton pressure for a very fortunate win.

As the final whistle blew, Sam Allardyce turned to his opposite number, offered his hand, and nodded a "Well played," saving his full thoughts on the opposition's performance for the postmatch press conference and the *Match of the Day* interview.

It had been a poor game, but as the supporters streamed away from the stadium, they did at least have the consolation of three more precious points.

Gavin Harris didn't hang around in the changing room. He was showered and dressed before the final whistle sounded and soon after he met up with Barry and Christina, along with hangers-on Bluto and Des, who continued to bask in the reflected glory of their famous friend.

Except that their famous friend wasn't feeling particularly glorious. He wasn't happy at being substituted and made sure his agent knew about it as they traveled down one of the escalators leading to ground level from the upper hospitality areas.

"If he's gonna pull me off like that, why did he bother paying more than eight million for me?"

Barry Rankin was always loyal to his clients, and he usually pandered to their inflated egos, but he wasn't beyond putting in a cautionary word when it was needed. "A little bit more effort might not go amiss, Gavin."

Christina was standing at Gavin's side. "And maybe a few early nights."

Her boyfriend ignored the caustic comment as, a little farther down the escalator, Bluto and Des burst into a very bad and very out-of-tune rendition of "Fog on the Tyne."

Gavin smiled but Christina sighed wearily. "I come all the way from London and I'm stuck with those morons."

"They're not morons," said Gavin. "They're my mates."

Christina shook her head, amazed that her boyfriend couldn't see the truth. "Gavin, believe me, they are *not* your mates."

They reached the ground floor and walked out onto the service road passing beneath the main entrances to the stadium.

As they went toward the parking lot, Barry spotted Glen emerging from another exit with Santiago.

Gavin and his entourage continued on, but Barry stopped and spoke to Glen. "Hello, mate. I suppose you've still got the needle about L.A.?"

Glen shrugged. "You were 'working,' Barry. I could hear the party in the background."

"Fair enough," said the agent, holding up both his hands. "I was partying. What can I say?"

"You can say hello to my friend here," said Glen, nodding toward Santiago. "He's the one you missed."

Barry stared. "Yeah? Well . . . what's he doing here in Newcastle?"

Glen smiled. "Santiago's on the books. See you, Barry."

They walked away, leaving Barry still staring.

16

Santiago never tired of soccer, or of training. He put everything he could into the next couple of weeks, knowing only too well that his time on trial was quickly passing. He felt he was doing well, but whether or not it was well enough was impossible to know. Praise didn't come easily from any of the coaching team.

Some days, when official training was over, he would work on alone. He would heave a huge string bag, bulging with twenty or more soccer balls, out onto one of the practice fields and line them up twenty-five or thirty yards outside the penalty box.

Then he would practice his free kicks, and he would go on practicing until every one of the balls was in the back of the net. And then, usually, he would start again.

One damp, gloomy afternoon, he was alone on the field. Dark, heavy clouds loomed overhead as he slotted one ball into the net and then walked back to line up for the next attempt.

Over in the reception area, Erik Dornhelm walked from the main building and stopped as he saw the distant figure preparing for the shot. He watched as Santiago took three short strides and curled the ball into a top corner.

Dornhelm's face remained expressionless. He simply walked to his car, got in, and drove away.

Santiago had arranged to meet Roz for a drink later that evening. And that was something else that was worrying him. They were getting on well, very well, and he wasn't looking forward to having to say good-bye if his trial was not extended. All he could do was continue to do his best. And hope.

He walked out of the dressing room and stopped at the large cork bulletin board, covered with various notices and team lists. His eyes scanned the board and rested on the team selection for the next reserve match, looking to see which of his training partners had made the squad. Hughie Magowan was inevitably there, and so was Jamie. And then . . . He read the name once and then again to be absolutely certain.

It was there. In black and white. It was there: S. MUÑEZ.

Roz was still on duty at the hospital when Santiago arrived. She was pushing a wheelchair containing a young boy with his leg in plaster along the corridor when she saw the beaming Santiago hurrying toward her.

"What are you doing here? Are you hurt?" She answered her own questions. "No, you can't be, you're smiling too much."

"I have some great news. I made the reserve squad."

"Yeah? That's brilliant."

"If the boss sees me do well, maybe he'll keep me on."

"I'm sure he will, Santi."

"So we celebrate tonight?"

"I finish in half an hour."

The boy in the wheelchair had been watching the conversation bounce back and forth as though he were at a tennis match. As it finally stopped, he took his chance. "Do you play for Newcastle then?" he said to Santiago.

Santiago was almost embarrassed to reply. "Yes."

The boy tapped on his plastered leg. "Sign your name on that."

Santiago hesitated. "You mean it?"

"Course he means it," said Roz, pulling a pen from her pocket.

When Roz finished her shift they went down to the quayside and walked across the Millennium Bridge to the Gateshead side of the river. It was still early; most of the bars hadn't even opened. But they were content to just walk.

"I phoned my grandmother while I was waiting for you. She was happy for me."

They were walking past the huge, glass-walled Sage Centre, as a group of young teenagers, talking soccer, passed by in the opposite direction.

"They'll all be asking for your autograph soon," said Roz.

Santiago still remembered what Roz had said in the pub on their first night out together. "Would it bother you? You never told me, what is your problem with footballers?"

"It's not footballers as such; it's the whole 'fame' thing. It's my dad's fault. When I was a kid, he was in a rock band. They had their five minutes of fame."

"Would I know this band?"

"I doubt it. The point is, some of the players remind me of him. One minute they're nice uncomplicated guys and the next, they're stupid rich idiots who walk out on their families."

They continued in silence for a few moments, both

deep in their own thoughts and memories. Santiago stopped and leaned on the railings, looking across the river, and Roz stood close by him.

"It was my mother who left us," said Santiago at last.

"She did? Why?"

Santiago shrugged. "My father never talks about it, but I remember his anger and his drinking. That's why I needed football so much, to get away from it, even as a kid. I always wanted it to be my life."

"So why did you have to come all this way to make it happen?"

Santiago turned and looked at Roz. "For that you have to ask the saints. Or maybe what the saints had in mind was for me to meet you."

Roz laughed. "Does that cheesy line work for you back home?"

"It sounds much better in Spanish."

Roz laughed again, but then they didn't say any more. Instead, they kissed, for the first time.

Mercedes was waiting for the right moment. Herman had eaten his evening meal and was sitting in front of the television, as relaxed as he ever was.

Julio looked at his grandmother, silently urging her to get on with it.

She took a deep breath. "I had a call from Santiago. He sounds very happy."

Herman said nothing; his eyes were still fixed on the soap playing out on-screen. Fantasy worlds were a lot easier to deal with than reality.

"Tell him about the game," said Julio.

Mercedes tried again. "He's playing tomorrow night, for the reserve team. After only three weeks! Fantastic, no?"

Herman still didn't look away from the screen and his voice sounded completely indifferent as he replied. "He left like a thief in the night without saying goodbye. Why should I care?"

17

THE RESERVES MATCH was being played under lights at Kingston Park, the stadium the team shared with the Newcastle Falcons rugby club.

In the dressing room, the veterans went through the same routines they'd gone through a thousand times before while the young players changed quickly and chatted nervously, knowing that both Mal Braithwaite *and* Erik Dornhelm would be out there watching.

Santiago was changing next to Jamie. "I wish Glen could be here tonight."

"Where is he?"

"In London. His son is getting married very soon. Glen has gone to meet the girlfriend's parents."

The reserves' coach, Bobby Redfern, came into the changing room and clapped his hands to get everyone's attention. "Howay, lads, pay attention, now. Claudio's hamstring is holding up all right, so I'll give him a run for at least a half. Santiago, I want you on the right flank—but keep tracking their number eight: He's as slippery as a bag of ferrets."

Santiago looked bewildered but Jamie smiled. "I'll translate for you when we get out there."

"Shut up, Jamie, and listen," said Bobby. "I want you to slot in behind the two strikers. And both keepers will get a half each. Right, let's get at it, then."

The players hung back, waiting for Bobby's all-too-familiar parting shot. "Oh, aye, and don't let them panic you into playing football!"

It was answered with a barrage of forced laughs and derision.

The tension and nerves of the moment made Santiago feel he needed a hit from his asthma inhaler. He waited as the others began to troop out and reached into his bag. As he took out his shin pads, the inhaler came out with them and bounced onto the floor. Quickly Santiago fell to his knees to retrieve it, but before his fingers reached the small blue cylinder, a size eleven shoe came down and crushed it underfoot.

Santiago looked up to see Hughie Magowan smiling down at him. "Sorry, pal. Was that important?"

There was nothing Santiago could do, but as he

walked into the glare of the floodlights his chest suddenly felt tighter—much tighter than it had before.

Less than a thousand spectators huddled together in small groups on the terraces; a few were die-hard supporters who never missed a match, but most were men, some with young sons, who just happened to live nearby and had nothing better to do.

Santiago struggled from the kickoff. The damp night air didn't help and soon he was gasping and wheezing like a twenty-cigarettes-a-day smoker. When he glanced toward the touchline he saw that Mal Braithwaite and Erik Dornhelm were already looking less than impressed.

Twenty minutes into the half, Hughie Magowan brought down one of the opposing forwards with his usual style and panache. The referee blew for a free kick and warned the big central defender that the next one would mean a yellow card.

Santiago was pulled back into the defensive wall. Magowan was standing next to him. He grinned. "What's happened to Speedy Gonzalez tonight? Lost the use of your legs?"

Santiago didn't have the breath to reply.

The free kick was poorly struck and cannoned off the wall. It was the perfect opportunity for a quick counterattack. Jamie played the ball cleanly into

Santiago's path but he had no pace; his legs wouldn't do what his brain was telling them. The speedy number eight Bobby had warned him about quickly overtook him and hooked the ball away for a throw-in as Santiago fell to his knees.

Jamie Drew came running up. "You okay?"

Santiago nodded and struggled to his feet.

Before halftime, the coaches and manager had seen more than enough. The number eight was running rings around Santiago, and even lumbering central defenders were; it was embarrassing.

As the ball went out of play for a throw-in, Santiago looked across and saw a sub stripped off and ready to come in. Bobby Redfern signaled to the referee and then beckoned to Santiago.

Slowly, looking as devastated as he felt, he walked off the field; he couldn't run. He touched hands with the sub and, as he went past Redfern, head bowed, the coach patted him on the back. "Get yourself an early bath, son."

Alone in the dressing room, Santiago slumped down on the bench, on the verge of tears. His big chance, probably his only chance, and he'd blown it.

He sat staring across the room, seeing nothing but reliving the nightmarish performance he had given out on the field. Mal Braithwaite walked in and immediately saw the despair etched on Santiago's face.

"What was that all about? Are you hurt?"

"No, Coach."

"What is it, then? Been out on the town?"

Santiago shook his head.

Mal hesitated for a moment. "Is there something else you want to tell me?"

Of course Santiago wanted to tell him. He was desperate to tell him. But he couldn't; it was too late now.

"No, Coach."

Mal sighed; he never relished this part of the job. "I don't know, Santi. You've got the skill, and I've seen the pace, but maybe you just don't have the stamina for the English game. Maybe you're best off playing back at home. I'm sorry, son, I have to let you go."

Santiago had to see Roz. To tell her. To let her know that he'd failed, that he'd let everyone down, that he'd been dumped. And that he was leaving.

He felt ashamed, humiliated, and he slunk away from Kingston Park while the match was still on. No one noticed him go, no one cared. After a performance like that, why should they? By tomorrow, he'd be forgotten; it would be as though he'd never even been in Newcastle.

Roz lived in one of the high suburbs clustered around and looking down toward the city center and the Tyne. When Santiago got out of the taxi, walked up to the door, and rang the doorbell, he expected Roz to open the door. She didn't.

The door swung back and Santiago was confronted with an attractive woman who was probably in her late forties but was doing her best to look a fair bit younger. The skirt was a little too short and the blouse was a bit too tight; Carol Harmison still saw herself as the rock-chick of twenty years earlier.

Her smile was genuine and welcoming. "Yes?"

"This . . . this is the home of Roz Harmison?"

"Roz! It's for you," called Carol, still looking at Santiago. "You must be the young man from L.A. I've heard all about you."

"Santiago, yes."

"Well, come in," said Carol, stepping aside.

Santiago nodded his thanks and stepped into the house. Carol closed the door. "I went there years ago, when my husband's band was on tour. We stayed at the Hyatt House on Sunset. They called it the Riot House in those days; you wouldn't believe the things we got up to. One time there was this—"

"Mum!" said Roz as she appeared on the stairs. "Aren't you meant to be meeting your mates at the Wheatsheaf?"

Roz had heard Carol's rock reminiscences before,

many times before. They could be entertaining and amusing, but were not for the fainthearted and most definitely not for a first-time visitor to the house.

"There's no mad rush," said Carol, casting an admiring, appreciative, and experienced eye over Santiago. Then she saw the look her daughter was casting in her direction. Words were unnecessary: The look said, *Get lost, Mum.*

Carol sighed. "But then again, I suppose they are waiting." She beamed at Santiago. "Really nice to meet you. You must come round again. I'd love to hear if L.A.'s the same as it was in the good old days." She grabbed a coat from a stand in the hallway and Roz ushered Santiago through to the living room.

"Great name!" called Carol as she checked her face in a mirror. "Santiago. So . . . evocative. Bye, then!"

"Bye, Mum."

The front door slammed, and for a moment Santiago stood looking at a display of framed gold albums and photographs of Carol with various rock bands. They made him think of Glen, someone else with their history on the wall.

"So what happened?" said Roz. "How did it go? I didn't expect you."

Santiago turned away from the photographs. "I was cut."

"Cut? Where? Show me."

"No, I was let go. Dumped. They fired me. I came to say good-bye."

"You're . . . you're leaving?"

"I don't belong here if I'm not on the team."

"But why? What went wrong?"

"I couldn't tell them. I couldn't say why I played so bad. I couldn't go to the boss and argue my case."

Roz took Santiago's hand and sat with him on the big old sofa that took up one side of the room. "Santi, I don't understand. What couldn't you tell them?"

"That I lied at my physical. To you. I have asthma."

"Why didn't you say so?"

"Because if I had, I wouldn't even have got a trial."

Roz was still holding Santiago's hand. She squeezed it gently. "Look, these things happen to young players all the time. You'll find another team."

"But not here. I was crazy to think I could make it work. And I've let people down. My grandmother. Glen. I'm going home, Roz. Tomorrow."

18

GAVIN HARRIS KNEW FULL WELL he shouldn't have stayed the night. But Christina had gone back to London and he was lonely and the two sisters he'd met in the club had been *so* welcoming.

He quietly closed the front door of the tower-block apartment, blinking as the harsh daylight penetrated his bleary eyes; he peered tentatively over the edge of the third-floor balcony walkway.

It was still there; his precious yellow Aston Martin was still where he just about remembered leaving it.

Gavin was not dressed for the daytime, and his full-length leather coat and black Armani suit looked even more out of place at the top of the run-down tenement block. He buttoned his shirt, yanked a beanie from his pocket, pulled it onto his head, and then took out a pair of wraparound sunglasses and slipped them on to complete the inconspicuous look. He looked about as inconspicuous as the yellow Aston Martin.

He found the graffiti-scarred elevator and pressed the button, just as a middle-aged woman in a head scarf walked by, heading for the stairs. "Doesn't work. Hasn't for years."

Gavin frowned; he was sure he remembered coming up in the elevator the previous night.

The woman stopped and looked back. "Aren't you . . . ?"

"No!"

But the woman wasn't fooled. "I can see why they took you off last week. You're shite!"

Gavin didn't stop to argue his case. He took the stairs two at a time and kept running when he got to the bottom. As he got close to the Aston Martin he skidded to a halt.

"Ohhh, *no*!"

The car was there all right, no problem. But the wheels weren't: The vehicle had been neatly propped up on four piles of bricks.

A couple of grubby-looking kids were sitting on the curb.

"Did you see . . . ?"

"Didn't see a thing, mister," said one kid.

Santiago comes on to play—and heads for the goal!

Roz cheers on
her boyfriend.

Gavin and Santiago celebrate!

A rising star on the team . . .

. . . but his dream may be over.

On the bench, waiting for his chance in the crucial last match of the season . . .

A nail-biting match for everyone watching . . .

Gavin in top form . . .

. . . goal!

Mobbed by their teammates as the final whistle blows . . .

"But we might know someone who did," said the other.

Gavin pulled out his cell phone. "Forget it." Wheels he could afford—by the truckload, if necessary. What he couldn't afford was another run-in with Erik Dornhelm. He punched in the number of a taxi firm he kept on the cell's phone book. "Come on . . . come on . . ."

"West End Taxis."

"I need one, urgent. This is Gavin Harris."

"Yeah," said the voice wearily on the other end of the line. "And I'm Clint Eastwood. Make my day."

"I'm *serious*. This *is* Gavin Harris. I need a ride, urgent. And I don't care what it costs."

The taxi was well on its way back to the city from Tynemouth. Santiago sat in the back, feeling totally miserable.

A sign on the dashboard read THANK YOU FOR NOT SMOKING, but it obviously didn't apply to the driver, who was puffing away happily and blowing the smoke out through the partly open window. At the start of the journey, he had attempted to chat with Santiago a couple of times, but got little response. He wasn't bothered; he was happy enough with his cigarettes.

Santiago had left a letter for Glen. It wasn't the way he would have wanted it; it seemed almost cowardly, but he couldn't face a humiliating phone call. So he had written the letter, explaining what had happened as best he could and thanking Glen for everything.

A voice crackled over the taxi radio. "Gordon, you anywhere near Blakelaw?"

"Aye, why?"

"Gavin Harris is stuck on the estate. Needs a car, desperate."

"But I've already got a fare."

"He's first team, man! Get there!"

Gordon looked at Santiago in the rearview mirror. "Sorry, bonny lad, detour. He's a celebrity, gotta get him outta there!"

Gavin was pacing anxiously as the taxi drew up. He wrenched open the door and immediately recognized Santiago.

"What's going on? You late for training, too?"

"No! I have to get to the station."

"Why?"

"I screwed up."

Gavin jumped into the taxi and slammed the door. "You can tell me about it on the way." He turned to the driver. "Come on, Jenson Button. Get us to the training ground."

Gordon the driver pulled away, not exactly as quickly as the top Formula One driver but burning rubber as best he could. As the vehicle sped toward the training ground, Santiago told Gavin the full story of the previous night's match, his asthma, and the crushed inhaler.

"So who was it who stood on the inhaler then?"

"Hughie Magowan, but it was probably an accident."

The taxi driver laughed. "I doubt it. Hughie Magowan's always been a nasty piece of work."

"D'you mind," said Gavin. "This is a private conversation."

"I feel sorry for the lad, that's all."

The cab pulled into the training-ground parking lot and Gavin grabbed Santiago's bag. "Let's get this sorted."

"But—"

"I'll talk to the boss."

He fished in his pockets for some cash as Gordon turned round. "So you're *the* Gavin Harris."

"Guilty."

"I have to tell you, you're—"

"Yeah, I know, I'm shite. I met your mother earlier and she told me."

"Well, the truth is, bonny lad, you're not worth eight million."

"Actually, it was eight point four million." He handed over a lot more cash than the ride had cost. "Keep the change."

The look that Erik Dornhelm gave Gavin and Santiago as he sat behind his desk and they stood on the other side like a couple of naughty schoolboys up before the headmaster gave absolutely nothing away.

But at least he was listening.

"The thing is, and with all due respect, gaffer . . . I mean, Mr. Dornhelm, sir," said Gavin, keeping the subject firmly on Santiago's situation rather than his own, "the club would be making a big mistake if they let this lad go."

"Oh, you think so?"

"I've played alongside him, and against him, and I can see he's got it. And so can the other lads. I mean technically, he's—"

"You mean he's better than you?"

Gavin hesitated. "Well . . . he's in that league. Or he could be. Last night he lost his inhaler. He's got asthma, see. That's why he was staggering around like Puff the Magic Dragon."

Dornhelm's eyes flicked from Gavin to Santiago. "This is true?"

"Yes, sir. I tried to hide it."

Dornhelm clicked his tongue with irritation. "Lying is a problem; asthma doesn't need to be. You can get treatment. Medication. Didn't your doctor back home explain this to you?"

"I didn't have a doctor back home, just the free clinic in east L.A."

Dornhelm paused, considering, and Santiago and Gavin exchanged a glance.

"People keep pleading your case, Muñez."

"All I want is the chance to prove them right."

"You think you deserve it?"

"I know I do."

Dornhelm almost smiled. But he didn't. Glen Foy, Mal Braithwaite, Bobby Redfern, and now even Gavin Harris had—one after another—told him that this kid had something special, something that needed nurturing and developing.

"See the doctor. Tell him about your condition. And then report for training."

Santiago couldn't hide his joy. He reached across the desk, grabbed Dornhelm's right hand, and shook it vigorously. "Thank you, sir! *Gracias!* Thank you." He turned to Gavin and shook his hand, too. "And thank you, Gavin. *Muchas, muchas gracias!*"

"No problemo, mate," said Gavin, guiding Santiago toward the door.

"Gavin!"

"Boss?"

"You stay!"

Santiago departed, all smiles, and Dornhelm waited until the door was firmly closed. "This is a decent thing you did."

"Yeah, well, he's a good kid, and—"

"But now please explain why you are dressed for a discotheque and are"—he checked his watch—"forty-seven minutes late for training."

19

GLEN NEVER GOT TO READ the letter; Santiago tore it up before his friend got home that evening. But he did tell Glen what had happened, and about his asthma, and about Gavin Harris's role in influencing Dornhelm's decision to keep him at the club.

Glen took the news philosophically. "You work hard and show Dornhelm what you can do and I reckon he'll see you all right now," he said.

He did. Santiago put everything he could into the next few days' training, and an impressive reserve-team performance was rewarded with an extended trial of a further month.

He celebrated with Roz. His fortunes were changing, and with the time pressure temporarily lifted, his confidence grew and he began to blossom. He became a regular in the reserves starting lineup and got his name on the score sheet for the first time in a match against QPR Reserves.

And there was an added bonus. Santiago was giving the QPR defenders such a miserable time that it became all too much for one of them. His frustration boiled over and he hacked the young player down with a tackle from behind.

As Newcastle players crowded around, the referee pulled out the yellow card and stepped quickly between the defender and Hughie Magowan, who was giving the offender a real tongue-lashing.

Soon after, the same central defender had the ball in space. He wasn't blessed with any great distribution skills; he was an old-fashioned stopper, like Hughie, and when he had possession of the ball, his natural instinct was to get rid of it. He didn't get the chance. Hughie came steaming in and flattened him.

The ref whistled and reached for his yellow card for a second time. "That was late, Magowan."

Hughie shrugged and held his hands up. "I got there as soon as I could."

The QPR trainer came running on to attend to his prostrate defender and Hughie strolled over to Santiago and winked. "He'll think twice about nobbling you again."

"But I thought you didn't like me."

"I don't, but you see that lass over there?" He pointed to a group of girls in the stand and one of them waved. "That's my kid sister, and she wouldn't like to see you hurt. She fancies you, says you remind her of Antonio Banderas, whoever he is."

Santiago laughed. "Does that mean you and me are okay?"

"What it means, Santiago, is that if you so much as touch her, I'll murder you!"

Santiago and Jamie Drew were forming a dynamic midfield partnership. In the game against Middlesbrough Reserves, Dornhelm and Mal Braithwaite watched and made notes as the two youngsters played an immaculate one-two and Santiago ran on to side-foot the ball past the keeper for his second goal of the match.

His growing fan club began to chant, and in the stand Glen smiled broadly. "Good lad," he whispered. "I knew I was right, I knew it."

Dornhelm seemed convinced, too. He almost smiled as he watched Santiago run back for the restart. "Good. Very good," he whispered.

The following day, Glen's prediction was proved absolutely correct when the trial period was scrapped and Santiago was given a contract until the end of the season.

———

The key turned in the lock and Santiago pushed the door open just a few inches. "Now you have to wait," he said to Roz.

"What?"

"I want it to be a surprise."

"You're crazy."

Santiago stood behind Roz and put his hands over her eyes. He pushed open the door with one foot, and then slowly led her through the open doorway and into the center of the room. "Okay," he said, removing his hands, "now you can look."

The spacious apartment was stunning, and so were the views from the picture windows of the bridges across the Tyne.

"Can you believe this?" said Santiago, standing close to Roz and gazing out toward the river. "A few weeks ago I said good-bye to the city and to you, and now I have a real contract and I move into this apartment."

"But . . . but how can you afford it?"

As Santiago started to answer, one of the doors leading from the main room opened and Gavin Harris emerged, wearing nothing but a towel around his waist.

"Gavin, say hello to my friend Roz," said Santiago.

Gavin feigned surprise at the sight of a female in

the apartment. "I didn't say anything about you bringing women here!" He grinned. "Just kidding. Nice to meet you, love. You're welcome, any time."

He went back toward the bedroom but stopped at the door and turned back. "Oh, and see if you can do something about his clothes, will you, love? The beach bum look might be okay in L.A. but I can't have him lowering the tone of the place now that he lives here." He laughed and disappeared into the bedroom.

"So that's how you can afford it," said Roz.

"He's a good guy. If it wasn't for Gavin, I'd be back in L.A."

"And he's earned himself quite a reputation since he arrived in Newcastle."

Santiago would hear nothing against his new friend. "He's a good guy, Roz. We're professionals; football is our life."

Roz went back to the window and stared out toward the Tyne Bridge. The sky was darkening and the lights were already beginning to illuminate the quayside. She was thinking of their first drink together at the Spyglass pub. And of her words of warning.

There was no problem in getting into the Club Tabu the second time Santiago arrived at the door. Not when he was with Gavin Harris.

The chief bouncer freed the velvet rope from its brass fitting and stood back. "Nice to see you, Gavin. How are you, gentlemen?"

"We're good, mate," said Bluto as he and Des followed them through the entrance.

The VIP treatment was all new to Santiago. "Fine. Thank you very much."

The club was hot and heaving; music pumped from the sound system and the dance floor was jam-packed with gyrating, sweating bodies. Gavin led his entourage straight through to the VIP section.

A second velvet rope was released by another bouncer and Gavin walked through to a long, blue-velvet banquette where Barry Rankin sat flanked by two young and very blond girls. A bottle of champagne was cooling in an ice bucket.

Barry, inevitably, was on his cell. "No, Colin, it would be a bad move, a very bad move." He waved at Gavin and the others as they sat down and then continued his conversation. "Look, Col, I wasn't gonna mention this but Valencia has been tracking you . . . Yes, for real. Sun, sangria, and señoritas. So patience, eh, Colin? You know I'm in your corner twenty-four-seven. Look, gotta go. Laters."

He flipped the phone shut. "Gavin! Dude!"

"This is my mate, Santi," said Gavin over the pounding music.

Barry indicated to one of the blonds to pour champagne and simultaneously waved to a waitress for another bottle. "How you doing, Santi? I hear it's going well."

"Yes, very good. Thank you."

"He notched a pair for the reserves the other day," said Gavin, like a proud big brother.

More miniskirted Toon teens began to cluster round the banquette, encouraged by the freeloading Bluto and Des.

As the waitress brought more champagne and fresh glasses, Barry leaned closer to Santiago. "You've got a contract to the end of the season, right? Who handled that for you then?"

"Glen. He handles everything for me."

Barry didn't hide his surprise, which was tinged with the slightest hint of disdain. "Glen Foy? Really? I mean, nice bloke, and I'm told a great player in his day, but what does he know about endorsements? And marketability?"

"I'm sorry?"

"Look, son, you make the first team and I can get you a Gap ad."

Santiago shook his head. "It's hot—I think I need some air."

He went outside. This *was* all new. All different. So different. As he stood looking toward the dark river and the bright lights, he suddenly felt homesick. He pulled out his cell phone and punched in a number. It was answered on the fourth ring.

"Hello."

"Julio," said Santiago in Spanish. "It's me."

"Hey! Bro! What's going on?"

Santiago smiled; it was good to hear his brother's voice. They chatted for a few minutes and then Santiago said, "Is Papa there?"

Herman *was* there, watching television while doing his best not to listen to the telephone conversation.

Julio put his hand over the phone receiver and spoke to his father. "It's Santiago, he wants to speak to you."

Herman looked up from the television screen and for a moment Julio thought that he was going to get up and come to the phone. But then he shook his head and went back to the TV. "Tell him I'm in the shower."

"Papa . . . ?"

"Tell him!"

There was no point in arguing. Julio lifted the telephone. "He can't talk now, Santi, okay?"

20

THE SEASON WAS DRAWING to an exciting and nail-biting conclusion. From the dizzy heights of the Premiership to the basement regions of Division Three, the final shakedown was beginning to become clear.

In the lower leagues, the first certain promotion places were claimed while some of the teams destined for the dreaded drop already knew their fate. Other clubs were battling for places in the play-offs.

In the Premiership, Newcastle continued to grind out results, with the prize of a Champions League place still tantalizingly close. But with injuries and suspensions playing their part and only two matches to go, that place was by no means certain and several clubs were still in with a shout.

Santiago had settled into the life of a professional footballer and everything that went with it. On the field, he had become a reserve-team regular and had turned in a number of eye-catching performances. Off the field, life was never boring; it couldn't be now that he was sharing an apartment with Gavin Harris.

Gavin seemed to look on Santiago as a particular friend. Perhaps it was because he could see that the young Latin American's friendship was genuine: There were no strings attached. He liked him being around, and if Santiago wasn't always quite comfortable with his friend's lifestyle, he didn't let it show. He was grateful to Gavin, he always would be, so he went along with it all and slipped into the Gavin Harris jet stream and found himself, at times, adopting his jet-set ways.

Many of the first-team squad appeared to have at least two cell phones with them at all times—they seemed to be as essential to the modern players as their soccer shoes. They were always using them: talking to agents, arranging endorsements, discussing ghostwritten newspaper articles.

Santiago had even imagined players out on the field with their phones clamped to their ears; wingers hurtling down the flanks as they discussed a new sponsorship deal, defenders going up for a high ball while arranging a photo shoot, keepers saving with one hand while clinging to that precious cell with the other.

So far, Santiago had just one cell, but carrying it around at all times was already becoming almost second nature.

He had changed for training and then gone to look at the bulletin board in the corridor to see the lineup for the next reserve-team match. His name wasn't on it; he wasn't even on the squad. He'd been dropped!

He couldn't believe it; he'd been playing so well and training so hard. He flipped open his phone, intending to call Glen, and realized that it had been switched off since last night. He powered it up and his voice mail informed him that he had messages.

He listened to the first.

"It's Glen. Haven't heard from you for a while. Hope it's going well. Give me a bell if you get a chance."

Santiago immediately felt guilty. He hadn't called for a few days. Was it a few days? Maybe it was a little longer.

The second message was from Roz.

"Hi. Just finished night school. It's ten past eleven; you're probably asleep. Call me tomorrow."

At ten past eleven the previous night, Santiago hadn't been asleep—far from it. He'd been out with Gavin, with his phone switched off.

Santiago made his mind up to call Roz as soon as training was over. He went to go back into the changing room to leave the phone in his locker, but saw Bobby Redfern approaching along the corridor.

"What did I do wrong?"

"What?"

"I'm not on the team; I didn't even make the bench. I don't get it. I play where you tell me, how you tell me, I score goals, I give a hundred percent and I get dropped."

Bobby Redfern smiled. "I didn't drop you, son. You're not available for selection."

"What? Of course I am."

"No, lad, you're not. You're going to Fulham on Saturday, with the first team."

Santiago's mouth dropped open; his breath caught in his chest. He leaned back against the wall and took a deep breath.

"You all right?" said Bobby.

Santiago nodded. "Yes. Yes, I'm okay. But I must call my grandmother."

"But it's the middle of the night in California."

"My grandmother won't mind."

21

THE FLIGHT IN THE CHARTERED jet took no time at all. One minute Santiago was settling into his seat fixing his seat belt and the next he was unbuckling the belt and preparing to get off. The plane just seemed to have climbed to its cruising height and then begun its descent—like a goalkeeper's clearance that goes directly from one penalty box to the other.

The directors, manager, coaches, and playing squad moved quickly from jet plane to luxury coach for the second part of the journey to Fulham, the part which would take the longest.

It was just routine for everyone else, but for Santiago it was another example of how his life had changed so much, and so quickly.

The traveling Toon Army of Newcastle faithfuls had traveled less stylishly but with equal hope, making early morning starts in crowded cars decked out with black and white, the colors of their favorite team. It was another crucial game in the push for that Champions League place, and there weren't many games left.

Those who didn't have a ticket, or couldn't get away, waited anxiously back in Newcastle as kickoff time approached.

Roz was at work: She had been unable to swap her shift; everyone wanted to see the match. And Roz would still see it, or at least part of it. She was the favorite nurse of a patient in a private room, an old boy called Mr. Ives, and he was already settled comfortably in his chair in dressing gown and slippers, eyes glued to the television set.

Roz put her head round the door. "Have they mentioned him yet?"

The old boy smiled. "Not yet, pet, it's just the warm-up. I'll keep you posted."

Glen was also preparing to watch the match on TV, settled on the sofa in his living room with a sandwich and a can of beer. As he took a bite from his sandwich he heard the first mention of his protégé as the match commentator and summarizer discussed the Newcastle squad.

"There's a makeshift look to the squad today, with all the injury problems," said the commentator.

"One of the subs, Santiago Muñez, is a completely unknown quantity."

The summarizer had been doing his homework. "Apparently he was discovered playing in a park in Los Angeles by Glen Foy, who was in the Newcastle team when they last won a major honor."

"Glen Foy!" said the commentator. "Now there's a name from the past."

In his living room, Glen took a swig from his can of beer. "Cheers, mate."

In the tunnel beneath the stand, the two teams and the subs emerged from their dressing rooms to take the field. There were the usual nods between those players who knew each other well from previous clubs or from international squads. There were a few jokes, a few good-hearted jibes, but it merely masked the tension that all the players felt.

Santiago was one of the last out, awed to be up close to all these Premiership players. Fulham's Steed Malbranque was standing opposite him and seemed to sense the youngster's tension. He smiled encouragingly and Santiago smiled back. And then they were walking out into the arena.

As Erik Dornhelm and Chris Coleman led their teams out onto the field, the stadium erupted into a barrage of noise.

The match was being bounced by satellite to scores of countries around the world.

In Santa Monica, California, it was early morning; palm trees were blowing in a stiff breeze as the second-hand truck Herman had bought pulled to a standstill in the parking lot of an English-style pub called the King's Head.

Herman climbed out of the vehicle and heard voices shouting as he looked at the pub. He walked toward the building and pushed open the door. The place was crowded with ex-pats, most of them wearing Newcastle or Fulham shirts. Many were eating fried breakfasts, which were being washed down with either tea or beer, even though it was just seven A.M.

Herman handed over ten dollars to the guy at the door and found himself a stool at the bar. He had never been in a place like this before, or heard so many hard-to-understand accents.

Three separate screens strategically placed around the bar were showing the game live from London.

The noise level in the bar dropped for a few moments and then erupted again as the referee blew for the kickoff.

Santiago was sitting at the back of the visitors' dugout with the other tracksuited subs. He was watching the match, but at times he had to just look around the stadium, hear the noise, feel the tension, to convince himself that he actually was there, and part of it all.

Newcastle didn't start well. Fulham pushed hard for an early breakthrough and the defenders in black and white saw a lot more action than their teammates up front.

At the hospital, Roz went back to Mr. Ives's room. "What have I missed?"

"Not a lot."

Roz sat on the edge of his bed. "How's your leg, Mr. Ives?" she said, her eyes fixed on the screen.

"It'll feel a lot better if we come away from here with three points, that's for sure."

Glen was watching with mixed feelings. He wanted the team to do well, a lot better than they were doing so far, but he wanted Santiago to get his chance as well. He got up from the sofa to fetch himself another beer.

Beer was flowing freely at the King's Head in Santa Monica. Rival fans exchanged good-natured banter as Herman watched, bewildered, wondering if he would get to see his son. By the time the referee blew for halftime, the Newcastle supporters knew that their team was fortunate to still be in the match.

In his living room, Glen listened to the halftime analysis as the match commentator sought the views of his summarizer, a former player. "Newcastle has been on the back foot for most of the first half, Paul, so what do you think Erik Dornhelm is telling them?"

"Keep it tight at the back, and see if they can nick one on the break."

Familiar football clichés, not rocket science, but accurate all the same. The way Newcastle was playing, the best they could hope for was a breakaway goal.

Glen got up from his chair. "Just one more beer."

Fulham was unlucky not to take the lead during the first part of the second period. Twice they went agonizingly close, as Shay Given performed heroics between the posts.

Dornhelm knew he had to change things and ordered two of his subs to get ready to go on.

The ball went out of play and the television camera zoomed in on the Newcastle bench, and Herman got the first glimpse of his son.

But he wasn't coming on; he was still at the back of the dugout as two other subs replaced teammates who trudged off with that disbelieving look of "Why me?"

Herman was as disappointed as Glen and Roz and even old Mr. Ives. "Thought we might get to see your boyfriend. They need someone to shake 'em up."

The double change did improve things. Newcastle began to see more of the ball and their first clear-cut chance came when a header ricocheted off the goal-posts and back into open play.

Newcastle still had the ball, and as it was swung over from out wide, a whole clutch of players went up for the header. There was an accidental but nasty clash of heads and a Newcastle forward went down in a heap.

Blood was flowing from the head wound and both Dornhelm and Braithwaite knew that there was no way their player could carry on.

"Muñez!" shouted Erik Dornhelm.

Santiago didn't respond; he was watching the injured player being led from the field.

"Muñez! Warm up!"

Santiago stared: He was going on!

22

HERMAN LEAPED TO HIS FEET as he saw Santiago cross himself and run onto the field.

"That's my son!"

Every face in the bar turned toward the proud dad.

"Are you serious?" said one Geordie with a half-finished pint of Newcastle Brown in one hand.

"Yes! That is my son, Santiago Muñez. I am his father, Herman Muñez!"

"Well, if he scores, Herman, I'll buy you a pint."

As Glen finished his third can of beer, he was feeling just as proud as Herman was all those thousands of miles away.

"Quite a day for this young man," said the television commentator. "His first game in the Premiership and his team is desperate for points. Talk about a baptism of fire."

In the hospital, Roz could barely watch. Her hands were gripping the bedclothes so tightly that they were almost sliding off the bed.

"Hey, I've got to get back in that bed later on," said Mr. Ives, seeing the scrunched-up bedding.

"Sorry," said Roz. "Come on, Santi, show them what you can do."

But showing what he could do was not going to be easy. Santiago was tightly marked and the few touches he got had to be played diagonally or back to his own defenders.

The clock was ticking and on the bench Erik Dornhelm checked his watch. A single point wouldn't be enough.

In the middle of the park, Santiago suddenly robbed a Fulham midfielder. The beaten player made a grab for Santiago's shirt, but was shaken off. Santiago was away out wide. He beat a defender and then cut back inside, closing on the penalty area. His strikers were calling, pointing to where they wanted the ball delivered.

The whole crowd stood up, almost as one.

In Santa Monica, Herman stood up.

In his living room, Glen stood up.

In the hospital, Roz stood up, and so did Mr. Ives, against doctor's orders.

Santiago feinted to pass, but then went on, the ball seemingly glued to his feet. He went into the box and the goal beckoned; he pulled back his right foot to shoot and then . . . a crunching tackle sent him crashing to the ground.

There was a moment of stunned silence, and as the Newcastle players turned to protest and the Fulham team looked on in horror, the referee's whistle sounded loud and piercing as he pointed to the penalty spot.

"Yes!" yelled Glen.

"Penalty!" yelled Roz.

"He's not bad, that boyfriend of yours," said Mr. Ives.

In Santa Monica, Herman just stared as the Newcastle supporters in the pub cheered and the Fulham faithful bawled, "Never a penalty! Never."

But it was. On the field, three Newcastle players pulled Santiago to his feet, patting his back and ruffling his hair as Gavin Harris collected the ball and placed it on the penalty spot.

"Oh, no," said Mr. Ives to Roz. "I can't watch if that playboy's taking it."

But with Alan Shearer nursing a slight thigh

strain, Gavin had no intention of letting anyone else near the ball.

Both sets of outfield players gathered at the edge of the box, and the crowd fell silent.

Gavin eyed the ball and then the keeper and then the ball again. He took three short strides, sent the keeper the wrong way, and neatly tucked the ball into the opposite corner of the net.

All his previous failings were forgotten, if only temporarily, as he was mobbed by his teammates and the Newcastle supporters chanted his name.

In the King's Head in Santa Monica, more than half the customers were jubilant, while the others stared into their beer and moaned about injustice.

The big Geordie who had spoken to Herman earlier got up from his seat and went over to the bar. He wrapped one arm around the beaming Herman. "You can have that drink, now."

"It's a little early for me."

The Geordie squeezed his new friend, almost forcing the breath from him. "Not in Newcastle it isn't."

The late goal had taken the sting from Fulham's play. They pressed but seemed to realize that for all their effort, today was just not going to be their day.

It wasn't. The final whistle sounded and the Geordie fans erupted.

Santiago clenched both fists with joy and Gavin

ran over and slapped him on the back. "Well played, mate."

Santiago didn't want to leave the field, it felt so good, but reluctantly he joined the twenty-one others as they trooped off, shaking hands and exchanging a few words with teammates and opponents.

Dornhelm was on the field. He went to Santiago as he approached, put an arm around his shoulder, and they turned and walked toward the tunnel together. Santiago felt unbelievably proud. Praise from his manager at last.

Dornhelm put his head close and spoke quietly. "What did you notice when you lined up that shot?"

"I noticed the goal," Santiago replied, confused.

"You should have noticed the two players who were in better positions than you. But you don't pass, you go for glory all the time."

He walked on, leaving Santiago crestfallen. What did he have to do to please this man?

The lounge was crowded with players from both teams as they enjoyed a postmatch drink with girlfriends, celebrity guests, and the usual batch of hangers-on.

But Santiago no longer felt like celebrating. He was still smarting from Dornhelm's rebuke, even though Gavin was doing his best to console him.

"Just forget about it, man. The gaffer does that to

everyone. You did great, everyone saw that. I'll get us a drink."

He moved off toward the bar, leaving Santiago to his thoughts, which were mixed. The day had been magical, unbelievable, until his manager had ruined it with those few short, stinging words.

As Santiago decided he had to shake it off, just as Gavin said, he felt a tap on one shoulder.

He turned round, and came face-to-face with David Beckham.

The world's most famous soccer player looked as cool and stylish as ever. He was smiling. "Santiago," he said.

Santiago's jaw dropped. He tried to speak but the words wouldn't come so he just managed a "Hey." Beckham must have been used to the effect his mere presence could have and he went on to save Santiago from embarrassment. "Congratulations, you were amazing today."

Santiago nodded nervously. "Oh, thanks!" he said at last. "My whole family are mad Real Madrid fans. My grandma, she loves you."

"Well, carry on playing like that, you'll be there one day," Beckham replied.

Santiago smiled, and then Beckham offered his hand and they shook.

"See you around," Beckham said as he turned to go.

"Nice to meet you," Santiago responded, still awe-struck.

Beckham went over to where two other immaculately dressed men were waiting. Santiago's eyes widened as he realized they were Beckham's Real Madrid teammates, Zidane and Raúl.

Gavin returned with the drinks.

"You see who that was?" said Santiago, still staring. "And who he's with?"

"Yeah, they're over here shooting a commercial. *Mucho dinero,* Santi." He handed Santiago a glass. "Come on, drink up and we'll get out of here."

"Where are we going?"

Gavin smiled. "This is my town, son."

23

THE PRIVATE PARTY was in the vast presidential suite of a hotel in the heart of London. Huge glass doors led to a balcony with panoramic views of the city.

Santiago was finding it all a bit overwhelming, an unreal end to an unreal day. He was tired; all he wanted to do was go back to Newcastle and to Roz. But Gavin was his friend, and Gavin wanted to party. So they were partying, big time.

A lavish buffet, which had remained virtually untouched, was spread across several tables, champagne appeared to have been delivered by the crateload, music was blaring out, and most of the females present looked as though they belonged on the catwalk.

Christina was there, but had shared no more than a few words with her boyfriend. Gavin, as always, was in demand. Gavin was everyone's best friend. Gavin was *número uno*.

Three girls who looked like models and a couple of guys in expensive suits were hanging on his every word as he outlined how the pressure of penalty-taking "just never got to him." Santiago hovered uncomfortably nearby, and then chief hanger-on Bluto called from across the room. "Gavin, over here! You, too, Santi!"

Gavin was always happy to indulge his friends, and with Santiago in tow, he followed Bluto into an adjoining bedroom. A huge, oyster-shaped bed, covered with a pink satin quilt, dominated the garishly decorated boudoir.

"Park yourselves on there," said Bluto.

"What for?"

"I wanna get your photo, a memento of today," said Bluto, pulling out a digital camera.

Gavin obligingly sat on the bed and Santiago sat next to him. From out of nowhere three girls wearing nothing but underwear—expensive underwear—suddenly appeared and draped themselves over the two footballers.

One perched on Santiago's knees, the second on Gavin's, and the third leaped onto the bed and poured champagne over the two players' heads.

The camera flashed, and as Santiago struggled to free himself from the unwanted attentions of the girl on his lap, he saw Christina appear in the doorway. She shook her head, sighed, and walked away.

Ten minutes later, Santiago emerged from the bathroom, having toweled himself off as best as he could.

The music was pumping out even more loudly and Gavin, completely unconcerned by the fact that he was still dripping with champagne, was dancing with Bluto. It wasn't a pretty sight, especially when, urged on by his friend Des and other revelers, Bluto started to do a striptease.

Slowly he unbuttoned his shirt, each button getting a louder cheer. By the time the shirt was pulled out from his trousers and his pale, flabby belly flopped into full view, Santiago had seen more than enough. He walked over to the glass doors and stepped out onto the balcony.

Christina was there, staring out toward the lights of the West End. "Not your kind of party?"

"I never know what to say."

Christina smiled. "You don't need to say much to most of the girls in there."

"But I have a girlfriend. Well, I think I have. I met someone I like a lot."

"She's a lucky girl."

The cheers from inside were getting louder; Bluto's performance was obviously going down well.

"And you and Gavin?" said Santiago. "How did you meet?"

"A party, pretty much like this one. Same sort of people: musos, models, footballers. He's gone a bit crazy since it all happened for him; now he's a superstar."

The words hit home, and Santiago thought of Roz and the things she had said to him. But he wanted to stick up for his friend. "Look, he's a good guy. If it wasn't for Gavin I wouldn't be here."

"I know," said Christina. "Basically he's a great guy. I just wish I'd met him when he'd grown up."

There was a huge round of applause and raucous cheers from inside the suite, suggesting that the Bluto show had reached its inevitable, gruesome conclusion.

Christina leaned forward and kissed Santiago on the cheek. "I'm leaving. Don't tell him I've gone—not that he'd notice, anyway."

24

THE HEADLINE SCREAMED: A NIGHT ON THE TOON!

It was splashed across the front page of the *Sun,* plastered above an accompanying photograph: Santiago, drenched in champagne, a girl on his knee, sitting next to another man, whose face was obscured by the girl draped over him.

The brief but graphic report named Santiago, Newcastle United's new wonder kid, but teasingly omitted the other player's name, referring to him only as a famous first-teamer.

Santiago was standing in Erik Dornhelm's office at the training ground and the newspaper was lying on the manager's desk.

"You want to explain this?" said Dornhelm.

"There's nothing to explain. It was just people fooling around at a party and—"

"When you travel with this club you are an ambassador for the club!" said Dornhelm, more loudly than Santiago had ever heard him speak before.

"Mr. Dornhelm, it's not my fault someone took a picture."

It wasn't difficult to work out what had happened. Bluto, Gavin's so-called friend and Saturday night dancing partner, had sold the photograph. He no doubt realized that the good times with Gavin couldn't last forever and had decided to make a killing while he could.

"It *is* your fault you exposed yourself to this kind of situation," said Dornhelm. He picked up the newspaper. "Who's the other player?"

"Excuse me?"

Dornhelm brandished the newspaper under Santiago's nose. "It says here there are two Newcastle players. Who is the other one?"

Santiago took a deep breath. "I'm sorry, Mr. Dornhelm, I cannot tell you that."

"You mean you won't tell me."

Santiago said nothing and Dornhelm hesitated for a moment, then threw the paper onto his desk. "Get out of here."

Facing up to Dornhelm had been bad enough, but Santiago was even more worried about what Roz would have to say.

He hurried to the hospital and found her pushing Mr. Ives down the corridor in a wheelchair. The cold stare Roz gave Santiago as he approached was not encouraging.

"Roz, I have to explain about that picture."

"What picture?"

"The one in the *Sun*."

"I don't read that rag."

"Then you didn't see it?"

Roz glared at him. "I've seen it!"

Mr. Ives was enjoying the exchange, waiting for his chance to join in. "I showed her it. I always have the *Sun*."

"It wasn't how it looked!" said Santiago to Roz. "What they say, it's not true."

"Santiago, I don't want to talk about it. I've got more serious things to worry about. Like your friend Jamie."

"Jamie? What about Jamie?"

Roz's face changed from a look of anger to one of concern. "He was injured on Saturday. Badly injured. While you were posing for team lineups, he was in here."

Jamie was in a treatment room. There were electrodes wired to his right knee and he looked pale and anxious as Santiago walked in. But his face brightened immediately when he saw his friend. "Great game on Saturday, mate."

"Never mind that—what happened?"

"Bad tackle. And I twisted it as I went down. They sent me here for an MRI."

"What does that mean?"

"Magnetic resonance imaging," said Jamie carefully. "Although players reckon it stands for 'Maybe Really Injured.'"

Jamie didn't laugh at the joke, and neither did Santiago.

"You'll be fine. They can fix anything these days."

Jamie looked at the electrodes fixed to his knee. "It felt bad when it happened. I could tell." He forced a smile. "Might have to give those salsa lessons a miss for a while."

Santiago stayed with Jamie until he was ordered to leave and then went searching for Roz again. Her shift was almost over.

"What does the doctor say about Jamie?" said Santiago.

"His meniscus is shattered. And there's a tear in the lateral cruciate ligament."

Santiago frowned. "Just tell me, Roz. Will he play again?"

"Not if he wants to walk again."

When Santiago returned to the apartment he found Gavin engrossed in a PlayStation game connected to the plasma TV. Both his hands were wrapped around the controls and his eyes were fixed on the screen.

Santiago's mind was still full of what he had seen and heard at the hospital. He went through to the kitchen to make a drink.

Gavin called to him, without looking away from the TV. "Thanks for covering for me, mate!"

"What?"

"The photo. Thanks for not telling the boss it was me."

"So, we're even! I don't owe you no more favors."

"Nope! No one owes no one any favors."

Suddenly Santiago was angry. Jamie's career-ending injury; the way Roz had looked at him when he blurted out his excuses for the photograph. The whole sad Gavin Harris lifestyle was put into perspective. Santiago went back into the other room. "You don't get it, do you? You're screwing up your life. You lost Christina and you sit there playing a stupid game."

"She'll be back."

"No, she won't! She can't stand what you're doing, or the guys you hang around with. How d'you think that picture got in the paper? Bluto sold it!"

If Gavin was bothered by Santiago's revelation he didn't let it show. He just kept pressing the PlayStation controls and, on screen, his Ferrari took the lead in the Monaco Grand Prix.

Santiago went to the TV and wrenched out the connecting leads and the TV screen went fuzzy. Gavin stared at him for a moment, but said nothing. Then he threw the game control onto the floor, got up, and went into the kitchen.

As Santiago followed, Gavin pulled back the fridge door and found a fresh carton of milk. Santiago watched as he struggled to open the carton.

"You think I'm some beaner who doesn't know stuff? I'm from L.A.! I know things! I've seen things! Things you've only seen in movies!"

"Why do they make these things so difficult to open?" said Gavin without looking at him.

"Listen to me! These are the best years of our lives, and how many we got, ten if we're lucky? Less, if we get hurt, like Jamie. Don't throw it away, Gavin!"

Gavin finally prized apart the top of the carton, spilling much of the contents onto the countertop in the process. But instead of drinking, he stood and stared directly ahead, as though he was considering everything he had heard. He nodded and then turned to face Santiago. "You know what? Why don't you piss off?"

He took a long drink and when he looked at Santiago again, a thin stream of milk ran from one corner of his mouth to his chin. "Go on. Get out."

Santiago turned and walked away. The front door slammed and Gavin took another drink of milk. He swallowed it slowly but he didn't look happy. There was a sour taste in his mouth.

25

JULIO HAD STARTED HELPING his dad out on weekends and on some nights after school. He didn't like gardening any more than his big brother had, but he liked the few dollars the work brought in.

They didn't talk much when they worked, but then Herman had never been much of a talker. He just got on with the job and expected those around him to do the same.

Julio had been clearing leaves with the blower. It was the job he liked least. You cleared a patch, you collected the leaves, you turned round and there was a whole new crop of leaves. He knew it would happen, but it wound him up every time it did.

Now the day was almost over and the fresh leaves on the driveway were partly hidden by the lengthening shadows cast by the garden trees.

"You can stay," whispered Julio as he glared at a leaf fluttering from lawn to driveway. He switched off the leaf blower, carried it over to the truck, and placed it carefully into the cargo hold. Any damage might be knocked off his wages. "Hey, Dad, come on! Grandma's gonna have dinner fixed by now!"

Herman had been working across the garden behind a stand of high bushes, finishing off his day by watering the expensive, specially imported plants the house owners particularly cherished. Herman may not have loved his work, but he was good at it, and conscientious.

As Julio stood back from the truck he was surprised to see a steady trickle of water flowing between the driveway and the lawn. Herman didn't like to waste precious water.

"Dad!"

There was still no reply. Julio walked across the lawn to the thick, concealing stand of bushes. He moved to one end and then through to a second, smaller lawn, surrounded by flower beds.

The hose was lying on the grass; the water spurting from it had formed a sodden pool. Beyond the hose, with his head and upper body crushing the precious flowers, lay Herman. Perfectly still.

It was a gentle training day. The season had been long and hard, players were feeling the strain, and coaches

184

knew from experience when to relax the routines. Particularly with the final match of the season just days away.

A few first-teamers and some of the reserves were playing a loosening game on one of the practice fields. Even Hughie Magowan was taking it gently, although it went against his nature.

For once, Santiago hadn't joined in, mainly because Gavin was playing and things between them were still strained.

Santiago was alone, jogging around the perimeter track. He didn't feel great. Not only was he hardly speaking to Gavin, but he also still hadn't made up with Roz. As he turned toward the main building he saw a figure he recognized. Glen.

Santiago increased his pace. At last, a smiling face.

Glen wasn't smiling when Santiago reached him.

"Hey, Glen. I meant to come over and explain about that thing in the paper."

Glen shook his head, and Santiago sensed that he was here for a very different reason. "What is it?"

"Santi, I had a call from L.A. You need to talk to your grandmother."

On the practice field, the game stopped as the players saw Glen wrap an arm around Santiago's shoulders and lead him off toward the main building.

"Something up?" said Hughie to Gavin.

Gavin shrugged. "Dunno."

The game restarted, but after a couple of minutes Gavin stopped running with the ball at his feet. "I'm gonna find out."

He hadn't been feeling particularly proud of himself since his outburst in the kitchen. But apologies didn't come easily with an ego like Gavin's. He walked off the field and Hughie followed.

"I thought you didn't like him," said Gavin.

"I've got used to him."

Glen was standing in the corridor, outside one of the offices. Through the glass window he could see Santiago speaking on the phone. And he could see the tears in his eyes. He looked away as he heard studded cleats on the tiled floor and saw Hughie and Gavin approaching.

"What's happened?" said Hughie.

"It's his father. Heart attack apparently."

"Is he gonna be all right?" said Gavin.

Glen sighed. "He's dead."

Maybe it was the news from America, maybe it was his conscience, maybe he felt that somehow and in some way he'd feel better for getting it off his chest, but something made Gavin go up to Erik Dornhelm as he stepped from his BMW.

"Can I have a word, guv?"

Dornhelm closed the car door and waited for Gavin to continue.

"I was the other bloke in the picture."

He knew he was telling Dornhelm nothing he didn't already know, or at least strongly suspected, and the manager's straight-faced reply confirmed that. "I'm shocked."

"And it was me who dragged Santi to the party. He didn't want to go, it's not his scene. He's got a good head on his shoulders."

"Why are you telling me this now?"

Gavin still wasn't quite sure. "I . . . I just wanted to set things straight."

Dornhelm looked over to a distant training field where a group of youth players and apprentices were playing. "These things happen. Girls, fights, parties. Every time I tell myself, they are boys. Boys with big bank accounts, but still boys. But this is not an excuse for you anymore. How old are you?"

Like a Hughie Magowan tackle, the reply was a little late in arriving. "Twenty-eight."

Dornhelm raised his eyebrows. "Twenty-nine, I think."

"Yeah, well, around there somewhere."

Over on the practice field, someone had scored, and Dornhelm could see the same sort of exaggerated goal celebrations that kids see on their television screen every time they sit down to watch a match. "The young players should be looking to you for an example, off the field as well as on it."

"I hear what you're saying, boss. And you're not the first person to say it."

Dornhelm nodded, apparently pleased that Gavin had shown enough courage to make his confession and maybe even think about changing his ways. He was about to walk off when Gavin came up with his parting shot.

"By the way, we were stitched up—that whole photo thing was staged. People like me are always being victimized. It's diabolical, and if I—"

Dornhelm sighed, shook his head, and walked away.

"What?' said Gavin.

26

THERE WASN'T TIME for a long good-bye, and neither of them could think of the appropriate words anyway.

The club had arranged the flight tickets quickly and without fuss, and Glen drove Santiago to Newcastle airport.

They parked the car and Glen waited while Santiago checked in. Then they walked to the departures lounge.

"This is it then," said Glen, knowing that his words sounded hollow and superfluous.

"Yes," said Santiago quietly. He'd felt numbed since the news of his father's death. Numbed, and helpless, and guilty, and angry, and overwhelmingly sad. For his father, for his grandmother and brother, and for himself.

Of all the ways it could have ended for him in England, it was ending like this. All he could do now was go home.

"Say hello to your . . . I mean, give my best to . . ." Glen was still struggling for words. "Just tell them I'm thinking of them."

"Thank you, Glen. For everything," said Santiago and he threw his arms around the man who had shown more interest and belief in his dreams than his own father ever had.

They embraced for a long moment and then Santiago turned and walked through to departures without looking back.

Glen watched until Santiago had disappeared from view. Only then did he wipe away the tears that were running down both cheeks.

Santiago sat in the departures lounge, unaware of everything that was going on around him, thinking of his father. The put-downs, the rebukes, the stubborn refusal to believe that his son could ever amount to anything more than a hired gardener.

It had always been that way, for as long as he could remember.

His thoughts went back to that long-ago night when they had fled Mexico. He saw the blazing searchlights again, cutting through the night. He saw his family, and the others, running from the border guards, up the incline toward the gaping hole in the high border fence.

He saw himself reaching the fence, bending to go through the gap, and the moment his precious, precious soccer ball slipped from his hands and went bouncing away downhill. He saw himself turning to chase after it and his father grabbing one arm.

"Forget it, it's only a stupid ball."

"Only a stupid ball," whispered Santiago. "Only a stupid ball."

"Sir? Sir, we're boarding now?"

Santiago looked up and saw a uniformed flight attendant staring at him. He had missed the flight announcement and the lounge area around his departure gate was empty.

"You need to hurry, sir."

Santiago grabbed his bag and stood up. He handed the attendant his boarding pass and started walking. Not toward the departure gate, but away from it.

Alan Shearer and Nicky Butt must have taken thousands of free kicks during their professional careers, but they still practiced them. Looking to bend the ball, power it, curl it, using instep or outside of the foot. There was always something to practice, develop, refine.

They were working together, watching each other, offering advice and comments. Nearby, Dornhelm and Mal Braithwaite were working with other members of the first-team squad, running through set-piece moves.

Dornhelm saw Santiago first; he just happened to turn in the direction of the changing rooms. He was jogging toward them, outfitted in full training gear.

Dornhelm watched and waited until Santiago came to a standstill in front of him, like a raw recruit reporting for duty.

"What are you doing here?"

There was a new sense of purpose about the young Mexican's reply. "I was sitting in the airport, okay? And I think to myself, now I got an excuse, a reason to give my buddies why things didn't work out. 'Hey, my dad died, I had to come home to take care of business.'"

The set plays had stopped, Shearer and Butt had stopped, and everyone was listening.

Santiago stared hard at Dornhelm. "You know why I needed an excuse?"

"No, I don't know," said Dornhelm.

"Because that's the way my father made me think.

He wanted to take away my self-belief, make it impossible for me to have . . . *aspiraciónes* . . . you understand that?"

Dornhelm nodded. "I understand."

"But I don't need an excuse! The only person who can tell me I'm not good enough is you! And then I might not believe you! *¿Entiende?*"

"Oh, yes," said Dornhelm. "I understand."

"I wish I could talk to him like that," said Gavin to his smiling teammates.

They watched as Santiago walked past them and over to where Shearer and Butt were standing with half a dozen soccer balls. Without waiting to be invited, Santiago broke into a run and curled the first sweetly into one corner of the net.

He walked back and hit the second into the opposite corner. Then the third, the fourth, and the fifth were dispatched with equal panache. No one said a word; they just watched. Finally, Santiago lined up for the sixth ball and struck it as hard as he had ever hit a ball into the roof of the net.

He turned around, his eyes ablaze, challenging Braithwaite or Dornhelm to complain. When they didn't, he stared from Butt to Shearer.

"Very good," said Shearer with a smile. "Now fetch 'em back, will you?"

———

"You do understand, Grandmother?" said Santiago in Spanish into the telephone.

"Of course I understand, Santi, there is no point in coming back," Mercedes replied. "What's done is done; it's God's will. Your father was too stubborn to say it, but I know he was proud of you. We all are."

Santiago wasn't going to argue with his grandmother about the pride his father had felt for his soccer-playing son. He had his views, she had hers, and it was best left at that. "I love you, Grandmother," he said.

"I love you, Santi."

Santiago put down the phone. He was back at Glen's house. He was happy to be there and Glen was happy to have him there.

He had tactfully gone outside while Santiago made the difficult phone call to Mercedes. But it had not been half as difficult as Santiago had imagined. She was completely understanding of her grandson's reasoning and decision, just as she always had been.

Santiago wanted to tell Glen about the conversation and thought he was coming back in as he heard the door open. It was Roz.

"Glen let me in," she said.

"Where is he?"

"Gone for a little walk. Can I stay? I'll go if you want."

"No. No, please stay."

Roz smiled and stepped farther into the room. She spotted the alcove with Glen's footballing memorabilia and photographs. "Reminds me of my place."

It was Santiago's turn to smile. "That's what I thought when I came to your house."

They fell into an awkward silence for a few moments, and Santiago gestured for Roz to sit on the sofa. He sat next to her.

"I thought you were mad with me. About the photograph in the paper."

"It doesn't seem important now." She looked at him. "How are you feeling?"

"Okay. I think. The worst thing is, I never made my peace with my father."

"He never made his peace with you, Santi."

Santiago thought about his father, seeing him as he had seen him so many times for so many years. Working, toiling in gardens, at roadsides, on scrub ground. Digging, raking, shifting leaves, cutting grass.

"I walked out on him; he never forgave me."

"You don't know that. All those pictures you sent home. Maybe he had one in his wallet."

The sky outside was darkening. Cold winds, heavy

gray clouds, biting cold, and piercing rain were no longer strange or unfamiliar to Santiago. "Home," he said. "I'm not sure where my home is anymore."

"I do," said Roz. "It's green, and it has goalposts at each end."

27

THE END OF THE SEASON was in sight. One game remained. One game that would determine the following season, and perhaps many seasons to come for Newcastle United. Champions League football wasn't just important, it was vital.

In the media room at the training ground, Dornhelm was talking tactics with the first-team squad as they watched videos of earlier games on a large plasma television screen.

Dornhelm froze the picture and pressed the REWIND button on the remote control. He froze the action again on a moment from the Fulham game and pointed to the screen.

"What were we thinking here? Who is picking up Malbranque? And who is covering Boa Morte, there?" He turned and nodded at two of his defenders.

"You two, you're too close; you're not married, you know."

Some of the squad chuckled while the two defenders squirmed in their chairs.

Dornhelm switched off the video and the TV. "We've had some good results, but everything rests on this last game."

"And it's only Liverpool," said a voice from the back.

"That's right, Liverpool. And if you leave them this amount of space you may as well pack your vacation bags now. Go and play golf in Marbella; don't bother turning up for the match."

Everyone knew he was right. They had shown only glimpses of the football they knew they were capable of for much of the season. But the season wasn't over until the final whistle blew.

"Question, boss?" said Alan Shearer.

"Alan?"

"Where's Santiago?"

"He lost a father. You saw how emotional he was. He needs time to heal."

"He'd heal a lot quicker if he was in the squad."

"That's right," said Gavin Harris. "And we could use some of his salsa moves if we're gonna crack Liverpool."

———

The players were not the only ones clamoring for Santiago's inclusion in the squad.

Since his performance in the Fulham match he had been the talk of Tyneside. In pubs and clubs, cafés and bars, the name Muñez was mentioned time and time again. He even had a record dedicated to him on local radio.

Newspaper opinions were mixed. Some columnists urged Dornhelm to pick the new whiz kid, while others were in favor of a more cautious approach, fearing that Muñez might be a one-match wonder. With so much riding on the outcome, they wrote, throwing the boy into the St. James' Park cauldron would be too much of a risk.

Everyone had an opinion, particularly at St. James' Park. From cleaner to parking lot attendant, from doormen to directors, everyone was convinced that they knew the secret to success on Saturday.

Dornhelm heard the voices, read the newspapers, and wisely kept his own counsel. Only one person would be selecting the squad for the last match of the season. That person was Erik Dornhelm.

Three days before the match he was working in his office at the stadium when he got a call from the head groundsman. His presence was required—urgently.

He walked from his office, took one of the escalators down to ground level, and went through a service tunnel leading into the soccer arena.

Far away to his right, a lone figure was on the field, practicing free kicks, sending ball after ball into the net. Dornhelm shook his head and stepped onto the turf.

Santiago stopped practicing and waited as Dornhelm walked up to him. "How you doing?"

"Okay, boss."

Dornhelm waited for a moment before continuing. "It's a tough thing to lose a father. I remember when I lost mine."

"Thank you, boss."

"You shouldn't be here," said Dornhelm, looking at the scuff marks in the grass. "The groundsman is having a fit. His turf is sacred."

"I'm sorry. I just wanted to see what it felt like to be on this field."

Dornhelm stepped over to the ball Santiago had placed for his next free kick and picked it up. "It's better when there are fifty-two thousand people watching. You'll see what I mean on Saturday."

Santiago nodded, and then he realized exactly what Dornhelm was saying.

"We're counting on you," said Dornhelm. "Now, get off the grass!"

At Foy Motors, work always slowed down as match day drew near. There was so much to talk over. Team selection. Tactics. Formations. They all had to be discussed and debated and decisions had to be made.

Glen could hardly complain; he encouraged it. And he was as fair in football as he was in everything else. He never claimed that he knew best, that he'd been in football for most of his life, that *he* was the professional. He listened, argued, reasoned, just like one of the lads. Because at heart, he *was* one of the lads. Maybe that was why he'd never made it to the top in football management. Or maybe it was just bad luck.

Foy Motors workforce and management had enjoyed their extended lunchtime discussion and had reluctantly, and not at Glen's prompting, returned to work. Glen was in his office and the others had their heads beneath the hoods of various vehicles when Santiago arrived. No one noticed, but Santiago was prepared for that. He went to an oil drum, lifted his arms, and pounded out a bongolike beat with both hands.

Somewhere, someone switched off the radio. Glen emerged from the office and Foghorn, Phil, and Walter appeared, as if by magic, wiping their hands on bits of oily rag.

"What's going on?" said Glen as he saw Santiago.

Santiago grinned. "I wanted you to be the first to know."

"Know what?"

"I'm on the squad for the Liverpool game!"

Glen clenched both his fists. "Yes!" He rushed over to Santiago and threw his arms around him.

"I told you!" boomed Foghorn, looking at Phil. "Didn't I tell you?" He turned back to Santiago. "First day we saw you, I said to Phil, that lad's got it. Didn't I, Phil?"

"No."

"I bloody did! Didn't I, Walter?"

"No."

"I bloody did!"

"You said he had no chance." Walter winked at Santiago. "Mind, he's always wrong. Good on you, lad."

Glen could hardly contain his joy; he hadn't felt this good since he had been pulling on the black-and-white shirt himself. "This calls for a celebration. Clubs, birds, booze!"

"What?" said Santiago and Foghorn together.

Glen laughed. "I'm joking! It's Blockbuster, shepherd's pie, and an early night for you, lad," he said to Santiago.

Glen's reputation as a chef was well known. "If I were you, Santiago, I'd skip the shepherd's pie," said Foghorn.

28

MATCH DAY. NEWCASTLE. The city a sea of black and white. From early morning, the tension and excitement grows. Banners hang over pub doorways, advertising the second-best alternative for those many thousands without season tickets: THE MATCH. HERE. LIVE.

There's no need to say which match; there *is* only one match for the Newcastle faithful.

The streets are clogged with traffic and pedestrians, all heading in one direction, to St. James' Park.

Santiago arrived early, to drink in the atmosphere. This time, when he walked through the underground tunnel beneath the stadium, he could legitimately step through the double glass doors reserved for players and officials only.

The doorman held back a door and smiled. "All the best, Santi."

Santiago nodded his thanks and walked on through another set of doors. This was it, the surprisingly small area of the vast stadium reserved exclusively for the actual business of preparing for the game.

Everywhere else there were offices, hospitality suites, media rooms, function rooms, corporate rooms, elevators, and escalators—long, seemingly endless corridors that snaked from one side of the stadium to the other.

But this part was different; this was the players' domain. Directly ahead of Santiago was the white-tiled tunnel leading out to the field. Halfway along the Astroturf-floored tunnel, some steps dropped down, and on the wall above were the words: HOWAY THE LADS.

To Santiago's immediate right was the match officials' dressing room, and farther to his right, the visitors' dressing room.

Santiago turned to his left, into the home team's dressing room. It was clinically clean. White tiles from floor to ceiling, light wooden pegs for hanging clothes, and benches of the same light wood. On the benches, perfectly spaced, was each player's uniform. Shorts, socks, neatly folded shirts. Santiago saw his own shirt. He couldn't touch it. Not yet.

A single treatment table was in the center of the changing area, and at one end a flip chart sat on a stand, waiting for the manager to turn any halftime tactical thoughts into artwork.

Through an archway were the showers and individual baths. Santiago smiled, thinking of the old photos he'd seen of footballers splashing about in huge communal baths.

The dressing-room door opened and Mal Braithwaite walked in.

"Blimey, lad, you're early."

But the time moved swiftly. Supporters bought their programs and squeezed through turnstiles. Those hovering outside jeered good-naturedly as they watched the Liverpool team coach bus, with its smoked windows, glide into the stadium access road.

Guests were arriving in the private boxes and hospitality suites.

In one of the boxes, Barry Rankin was enjoying a drink with a couple of local businessmen and their wives when the door opened and Glen walked in with Roz and her mom, Carol.

Barry feigned surprise. "Private box, Glen? You must know one of the players."

Glen just ignored the remark. Carol had dressed

for the occasion; this was just like old times. She was wearing a fake fur coat, which she took off to reveal a figure-hugging top and a leopard-print miniskirt.

She helped herself to a glass of wine and smiled at Glen. "This is the life. Reminds me of when Roz's dad was famous. They played stadiums like this. I'd be backstage with a Jack Daniels and a—"

"Mum!" said Roz quickly. "No stories, eh? Not today."

Carol shrugged and turned back to Glen. "So, Glen, you're single then?"

Glen reached for a drink of his own. "Aye, lass, and with every intention of staying that way. Got a son, though, and a daughter."

Glen's daughter, Val, was at that moment walking into the King's Head pub in Santa Monica with Santiago's grandmother, Mercedes, and his brother, Julio.

The pub was if anything even more crowded than it had been for the previous Newcastle match, but this time, the place was more evenly divided between those wearing black and white and those in the red of Liverpool.

It was noisy, hot, and heaving with unfamiliar-sounding voices exchanging jibes and predictions.

Val edged Mercedes toward one of the televisions, and as they moved closer Julio tugged at his grandmother's arm and nodded up at the screen. Santiago's name was there, listed among the Newcastle starting eleven.

"He's in," said Mercedes. "He's playing."

Julio grinned. "Of course he's playing."

Erik Dornhelm had given his final prematch pep talk and his players were about to take to the field. They were standing in the tunnel, nervous and edgy, ready to go out. Santiago was at the back. There was little banter, few words were exchanged; everyone knew what was at stake.

Suddenly they were moving forward, and as they passed beneath the HOWAY THE LADS legend, several of the Newcastle players reached up and touched the special words. Santiago did, too. He had to; there might never be another chance.

The sound of fifty-two thousand cheering voices was almost overwhelming as they moved onto the field.

Santiago gazed around the mighty arena, and as the coaching staff and substitutes took their places in the airline-style heated seats at the back of the dugout, he saw Jamie Drew, Hughie Magowan, Bobby Redfern, and most of the reserve-team players sitting a few rows back in the crowd. Jamie grinned and gave his friend the thumbs-up sign.

On the field, Santiago was adjusting to the incredible volume of sound sweeping down from the Toon Army banked around the towering stadium. Fulham had been one thing, but this was different—totally, incredibly different. Santiago's legs felt weak; his heart was pumping as he looked across to his left and saw Gavin Harris giving him a nod and a smile of encouragement.

Santiago knew he would feel better once the whistle sounded and he could just play, do what he had always dreamed of doing in the type of arena he had always dreamed of playing in. But the seconds passed agonizingly slowly as the referee checked his watch and looked across to his two assistants to ensure that they were ready to start.

In those few brief seconds, Santiago relived his amazing journey of the past years and months. The boy juggling a football outside the Mexican tenement, the young man shoving cardboard shin pads into his socks and dominating *Americanitos* games, Glen Foy waiting to speak to him by the battered old bus, his grandmother spilling his travel tickets onto the tabletop, and now this. Now this.

Up in the private box, Carol had reluctantly abandoned her wineglass and put on her coat and followed the other invited guests out through the doors to their comfortable seats.

As she settled herself between Glen and Roz she looked down at the two teams lining up far below. "Oh, I'm a great football fan," she said to Glen. "Who is it we're playing?"

And then the whistle blew, and the match began.

29

GORDON, THE TAXI DRIVER, was racing his cab through the almost deserted city streets. He had to get somewhere fast.

As he neared his destination, the taxi radio crackled into action. "Gordon, got an airport pickup for you."

Gordon flicked a switch. "Can't, Tommy, no way. I'm running an old lady to the artificial limb center. She's having a new leg fitted, so I might have to wait quite a while."

He flicked the switch and pulled the cab to a standstill. Then he jumped from his empty vehicle, locked the door, and ran across the road into the pub.

It was packed, but Gordon had a seat and a pint waiting for him close to the TV screen. Gordon was good friends with both Foghorn and Phil of Foy Motors.

He edged his way through the tightly crammed bodies and the clouds of blue cigarette smoke and threw himself down on his chair.

He picked up his pint. "How's it going?"

"We've made all the early running," said Phil.

Gordon took his first sip. "How long we been playing?"

"A minute," said Foghorn.

The early exchanges were hard fought and fiercely contested. For all the overseas players in both teams' ranks, this was an old-fashioned English-style, blood-and-thunder battle, like a one-off World Cup tie.

It was end-to-end stuff. Crunching tackles were going in on both sides, and before too long the referee reached for his yellow card and the first name went into the book.

Kieron Dyer was the unfortunate player. It could have been any one of a number of others, but the ref was making it clear that he would stand no nonsense.

Newcastle was pressing and Gavin Harris seemed to have lifted his game and was putting in his best performance in a Newcastle shirt. But as a move broke down up front, Liverpool counterattacked with their typical speed and precision.

The ball dropped for Harry Kewell on the edge of the box. He whipped in a shot which Shay Given did well to push out. As the crowd breathed a collective sigh of relief, Steven Gerrard came steaming in for an easy tap-in.

The stadium went deathly quiet, save for a small section high up away to the left of the dugouts, where Liverpool's traveling band of fans, called Kopites, were as delirious as their idols down on the field.

Up in the private box, Glen put his head in his hands, Barry chatted on his cell, and Carol looked forward to another glass of wine at halftime.

In the King's Head, Santa Monica, half the customers were up on their feet celebrating while the other half exchanged anxious looks with each other as they sipped their Newcastle Brown.

Mercedes turned to Julio. "It's not a problem. The second half will be better."

In the pub in Newcastle, Foghorn's voice boomed out louder than anyone's. "Glen's lad is doing well, though. I've always said he's good, haven't I, Phil?"

"Shut up, Foghorn," said Phil, finishing his beer. "And it's your round."

The remainder of the first half was played out at the same frenetic pace, and as the referee brought proceedings to a conclusion, Foghorn finally stood up to get the round in.

The television commentators and experts were ready with their first-half analysis.

"Most of the real chances have been made by

Liverpool, but Gerrard's goal is the one that separates the two teams at halftime."

"Talk about stating the bloody obvious," said Foghorn as he moved off with three empty pint glasses.

In the Newcastle dressing room, the atmosphere was subdued as the players and subs listened to their manager calmly and coolly explaining what he wanted and expected from them in the second half.

"You did a lot of things right, and I don't want to see any heads dropping."

He turned to their right back, Stephen Carr. "You're giving Kewell too much room on the flank, and we have to cut their flow off in the middle of the park."

As the players stood up to return to the field, Dornhelm was ready with his final words of encouragement. "Forty-five minutes," he said. "Forty-five minutes to take our place in the Champions League. Let's go get it."

30

THE SECOND HALF picked up at the same lightning speed as the first had finished, and as the minutes passed, Santiago's contribution to the match became more and more telling.

Santiago was not out of place, not for moment. This was where he was born to be, where he truly came alive. He quickly found the pace of the game and adjusted to the tempo. His early touches, speed, and agility caused problems for the Liverpool defense.

He was unknown to them; they had never played against him before, unlike the other Newcastle players whose particular special tricks and feints they could at least attempt to read or anticipate.

From one run out wide, Newcastle won a corner. Santiago ran into the box and jostled for position as Kieron Dyer set up the ball for the kick.

A curling in-swinger came over quickly and Alan Shearer rose majestically at the far post to head it back into the heart of the crowded box. Gavin Harris volleyed the ball from six yards, giving the keeper and defender on the line no chance.

The net bulged and the crowd went berserk. Liverpool players went hurtling toward the ref, screaming that they had been pushed or kicked. But the ref turned away and pointed to the center spot.

One–all.

Santiago was just one of the players mobbing the ecstatic Gavin Harris.

In the private box they were on their feet, in the city center pub they were on their feet, and in the King's Head, Santa Monica, half the customers were on their feet. The remainder were making exactly the same protests as the Liverpool players had made to the ref a few seconds earlier.

"You see," said Mercedes to Julio in Santa Monica. "I said we would be better now."

"*We,* Grandmother?" said Julio.

"Of course, *we*! We are Newcastle now."

But the joy of the newly enlarged Toon Army was short-lived. The song "Blaydon Races" was still ringing around St. James' when Liverpool retook the lead. The rows of journalists and radio reporters massed behind the dugouts were working overtime as they scribbled in notepads or yelled out the details to their listeners. This was developing into a classic end-of-season encounter, one that would be talked about for years to come.

Two–one to Liverpool. And now Liverpool, urged on by the hugely competitive Steven Gerrard, looking to put the game beyond Newcastle's reach, began dominating all phases of the play.

Santiago was forced to track back and help out in defense. He slid in a well-timed tackle but conceded a corner in the process.

By the dugout, Erik Dornhelm paced nervously, only retaking his seat when the corner was cleared. But it was still all Liverpool. Pushing, probing, going close with shots and headers.

Santiago was seeing more and more of the ball, though as an emergency defender more than as a creative midfielder. But the more he had the ball, the more his confidence grew. Suddenly he intercepted a Liverpool pass and, for once, found himself in a little space.

This was his chance to break. He set off like a greyhound, going past two defenders before sending a glorious cross-field pass to Nicky Butt.

The crowd roared its approval before the move broke down with a timely defensive back header. As the Liverpool keeper gathered the ball and the Newcastle players trotted back to face up, Alan Shearer mouthed a "Great ball" to Santiago.

It made him feel even better than he already did. Win or lose, this had to be the game of his life.

As the clock ticked on, the momentum of the match gradually swung in Newcastle's favor. They were playing the ball, capturing the midfield, thanks largely to Gavin Harris and Santiago.

Santiago was everywhere, looking for the ball, winning it, wanting it, demanding like he always had with the *Americanitos*. And he was getting it.

With fifteen minutes to go, the Liverpool defenders were panicked into conceding a free kick ten yards outside the box.

Nicky Butt gathered the ball and placed it a little in front of where the offense had taken place. The referee immediately nudged the ball back to the spot from where he wanted the free kick taken and then paced out the ten yards. The Liverpool players argued, but began forming their wall.

Alan Shearer and Nicky Butt waited, quietly discussing which of them would take the shot.

But on the touchline, Erik Dornhelm beckoned to one of his defenders and exchanged a few quick words. The defender nodded and then jogged over toward the penalty box. As the Liverpool wall settled, jostling the two Newcastle players who had joined their ranks, Santiago joined the cluster around the ball.

The keeper was ready, the wall was ready, and the referee was ready. He lifted his whistle to his lips and blew.

Shearer feinted to move but then stopped as Butt closed on the ball and tapped it sideways, into the path of the already moving Santiago.

He took six steps, hit the ball with his right foot, and sent it spiraling over the wall. Heads turned as the ball curved to the left; the keeper was already diving, his arm outstretched. But he was beaten and the ball flew into the top left-hand corner of the net.

As noise exploded in his eardrums, Santiago ran toward the goal line. The vision of *The Angel of the North* flashed into his mind and instinctively he flung his arms out on each side and stopped running to receive the applause, the cheers, and the adulation. A second angel of the north had announced his arrival.

31

"GOOOOAALLLLL!!!!!!" screamed Julio in the King's Head, Santa Monica, doing his own more than passable impersonation of the commentator Andres Cantor and bringing the other Newcastle celebrations to a halt as the Geordie ex-pats turned to look.

"That is my grandson!" yelled Mercedes, pointing at the screen. "His brother!"

Even the Liverpool supporters were staring now.

"It's true," shouted Glen's daughter, Val. "And he's from here!"

"Then you shouldn't be back there," said one of the Geordies. "Come up here to the front."

Chairs were moved aside and bodies shifted as Mercedes, Julio, and Val were ushered through to the front row and given the very best seats.

"I met the lad's dad," said the big Geordie Mercedes found herself sitting next to.

"What? How could you?"

"He was here. In this place, for the Fulham game. He was over the moon about his lad's performance. I bought him a drink."

Mercedes turned to Julio and Val. "You hear this?"

"Yes," said Julio.

"I'm so glad," said Val.

Mercedes looked up at the television screen. She could hardly see the picture; her eyes were too full of tears.

As Santiago jogged over the halfway line he heard the chant coming from the Gallowgate end. It was his name; they were chanting *his name.*

On the touchline, the fourth official appeared and held up the electronic board. The numeral 3 was glowing. Three minutes; they had just three minutes to claim a place in the Champions League.

"Come on, lads!" shouted Alan Shearer, turning to his teammates and clapping his hands. "Come on!"

Liverpool was not going to give it away. A point at St. James' in a crucial match such as this would be a massive achievement. And they might still just get it. A single point for the draw was of no use to Newcastle— they needed the full three points for a win—and in their efforts to find the winner, they could be vulnerable to a swift counterattack.

That was exactly what happened. As the Newcastle team pushed up, the ball was lost and Liverpool swept forward. A probing ball arced into the Newcastle half, and as the Toon Army held their collective breath, only an interception by the quick-thinking Stephen Carr averted disaster.

Defense instantly switched to attack and Gavin Harris collected the ball in space. He moved forward, drawing two players toward him, then sent a perfectly weighted pass across the field into Santiago's path.

Santiago took the pass in his stride, and a sudden burst of acceleration took him past and away from first one, and, as he cut inside, two Liverpool players.

The route to goal was opening up. Gavin Harris was steaming toward the box on one side of the field as Santiago ran on and on. But the defenders were chasing back, too.

Erik Dornhelm leaped to his feet as he watched Santiago close on the goal. "Pass," he said grimly, as memories of the Fulham game and training sessions came flooding back.

Santiago reached the right-hand side of the box and the keeper raced out to narrow the angle and smother any attempted shot on goal.

"Pass," growled Dornhelm, louder than before. "Pass!"

Santiago drew back his right foot, looking as though he was going for the shot. But then he sent a perfectly placed ball across to the far post for Gavin to complete the simplest of tap-ins on the run.

And Gavin didn't stop running. Not until he reached the corner flag, where he turned and was instantly smothered by every one of the Newcastle players, including the jubilant Santiago.

Cheers and screams and yells of delight rang and echoed around the stadium.

On the touchline, Mal Braithwaite was hugging Dornhelm. "He passed," muttered Dornhelm happily. "He passed."

In the Newcastle city center pub, Foghorn was hugging everyone he could get his hands on.

In Santa Monica, Mercedes was hugging her younger grandson, as half the pub shouted, "GOOOOAALLLLL!!!!!!" Amid the yells and celebrations, Val reached into her handbag, pulled out her cell phone, and began punching in a number.

In the private box, Roz was hugging her mother and Glen. And when Glen finally emerged from the madhouse, Barry Rankin was leaning across to speak to him. "We should talk about that lad."

"Talk about what?"

"Representation. He's got to be careful, Glen, there's a lot of sharks out there."

Glen smiled. "Oh, I know that, Barry. That's why Santiago's signed with me."

"What?"

"That's right, with me. You should remember that, next time you're in a Malibu hot tub."

Barry Rankin was upstaged even further when, for once, someone else's cell rather than his own began to ring.

Glen took his phone from his pocket and clamped it to his ear, struggling to hear as cheers continued to rock the stadium. "Hello? . . . Val? . . . What?"

The game wasn't over yet, though. Manager, head coach, supporters: Everyone was counting down the seconds as the final moments of the incredible drama were played out.

"Hold! Hold!" shouted Dornhelm to his players.

"Tight!" screamed Braithwaite. "Concentrate!"

The final minute seemed to last an hour. Liverpool threw every player forward as Newcastle dragged everyone back into their own half.

But then the referee checked with his two assistants and raised the whistle to his lips.

The traditional two short and one long blasts on

the whistle signaled the end of the match, the end of the season, and the longed-for prize of Champions League qualification.

Every Newcastle player on the field raised both arms in triumph as management and subs ran onto the pitch.

Santiago heard his own name being chanted as he stared, dazed, at the waving, moving ocean of black and white.

Steven Gerrard and then Sami Hyypia came across to shake his hand and offer their sporting congratulations. Gavin Harris ran over, lifted him off his feet, and bear-hugged away most of what little breath remained.

And when he was back on the ground and Gavin had run off to receive the congratulations of his manager, Santiago raised his arms again. As thousands of voices chanted his name, he turned to every side of the stadium, one after another. And waved.

32

GLEN HAD RACED from the private box, dashed down an escalator, out of the stadium, and back in through the players' and officials' entrance.

The doorman didn't attempt to stop him. No one tried to stop him; no one cared.

He went through the second set of doors into the players' tunnel and squeezed his way through the Liverpool players as they headed for their dressing room.

"Well played, lads," he said as he moved in the opposite direction. And he meant it. It had been an awesome game.

He burst out of the tunnel and saw Santiago just a few yards away. He was still waving to the crowd. "Santi!" shouted Glen. "Santi!"

Santiago heard the voice and turned. "Glen!" He ran over, ready to embrace the man who had turned his seemingly impossible dreams into reality.

But before Santiago could throw his arms around his friend, Glen thrust his cell phone toward him. "Someone needs to speak to you!"

"What?"

"Take the phone, Santi!"

Santiago grasped the phone in his trembling hand and pushed it to his ear. "Hello?"

The King's Head in Santa Monica was rocking as the Newcastle Brown flowed, but Mercedes shouted to make certain her grandson heard what she had to say. "Santiago! We saw the game! Julio and me. Glen's daughter brought us. You were fantastic. And I must tell you something else. About your father."

"My father?"

As the celebrations went on in St. James' and in Santa Monica, Santiago listened to the story his grandmother had to tell. He just nodded as he listened, his heart thumping and tears coming to his eyes. When he tried to speak, his voice caught in his throat. Finally he managed to blurt out, "Thank you, Grandmother. Good-bye."

He shut down the phone and handed it back to Glen.

"When I played in the Fulham game, my father saw me. He went to watch me play," he said softly.

Glen nodded. "Aye, lad. And I reckon he is probably watching you right now."

He threw his arms around the young player and then turned him toward the private box high up in the stand and pointed.

Roz was waving. When she saw that Santiago had spotted her, she blew him a kiss.

Fifty thousand Geordie voices were now shouting and singing their praises.

Santiago looked up at the stands and the massed ranks of black and white, and then his eyes turned back to the green of the field and the goalposts at either end.

Roz was right.

This was home.

He punched the air in triumph.